CW00858822

To the lovely Lisa

Hope you enjoy it.

Bill x

1

The Adventures of Jamie McGregor

Jamie and the last Dragon

W G Walker

CHAPTER ONE

An Unexpected Journey

It was the school holidays and Jamie was more excited than usual. The reason for the extra excitement was that Jamie's Grandad was coming. Jamie's parents had invited Grandad down to stay with them the plan being, that Grandad would help to look after Jamie while his parents had still to work. Although at 12 years old, Jamie was not exactly a child. Jamie's parents considered him too young to be alone all day.

Jamie was quite tall and skinny for his age. He had a mop of blonde hair with just a hint of red in it. He had a fresh face with cheeks that turned red at even the slightest hint of embarrassment. He also had a small sprinkling of freckles on his nose. His favourite clothes were jeans and tee shirts or sweatshirts with trainers. He had one particular favourite tee shirt that had emblazoned across it the logo of a rock band he liked. It was black in colour and it had a pale cream coloured skull which, had wings coming out from each side. There was a motor cycle wheel underneath and encircling this, the words 'The Flying Brimstone Brothers.'

The last time that Grandad visited them was months ago. His arrival then caused complete havoc in the street by arriving by hot air balloon. He managed to demolish half of the street's chimney stacks, before he finally landed the thing by smashing through Mrs Perkins new sky light window in her bathroom and she was taking a bath at the time. You could hear her screams for miles.

Jamie's Grandad was no ordinary fellow. A gentle stroll in the countryside with him could turn into a serious expedition with all manner of adventures. A polite conversation would turn into an epic story of Biblical proportions and he could do the most amazing tricks with that old walking stick of his. Unknown to Jamie at this time was that Jamie's Grandad belonged to a secret international organisation. The organisation was called The International High Council for the Investigation of Unusual Phenomena or I.H.C.I.U.P. for short.

It was a place where people did research, not the kind of research that you could undertake at 'normal' Universities or Colleges. As for the subjects under study, you would not find them on any prospectus. The people who studied there were very unusual also. They were the people to whom Governments turned for help when they did not know how to deal with a serious and very often dangerous situation involving strange events. For example, suppose your home was taken over by an angry Leprechaun who had turned your dad into a mouse and your mother into a goat. Or imagine a huge mythical Cyclops monster from ancient Greek mythology suddenly appeared in your town and was eating people. Who would you call to help you? The Police would not have a clue what to do. Imagine the scene. You try to phone for help. You dial the emergency code number 999 and the operator asks "Which service do you require, Police, Fire Brigade or Ambulance? And you say… "Hello operator my mother has been turned into a goat and my dad into a mouse so can you send someone to help?" Or "There's a huge Cyclops running around and he's eating people send help quickly." The reaction of the operator would be to give you a sound telling off and to stop wasting their time or you'll be in serious trouble. Or even try running into a police station and say to the Police "Help, a mad Leprechaun has taken over my house and turned my parents into animals." The Police would probably run you out of the station or lock you up. Jamie's Grandad and the other members of the high council are people who would know exactly what to do. They are the very people who deal with such problems. Clear up the mess with no fuss and make everything go back to normal and make it look as though nothing had ever happened and keep it very, very quiet and very, very secret.

Jamie's Dad went to collect Grandad from the train station and while he was away, Jamie's Mum had a quick word with Jamie. "I want you to promise me that you will behave. Don't encourage your Grandad in any way. He's bad enough as it is but when he has an appreciative audience like you he goes completely over the top with his fanciful stories and his magic tricks."

"I like his magic tricks. They are so cool," replied Jamie. Jamie's Mum thought for a few seconds and grin appeared on her face... "Yes...they are, but, try to keep him away from the neighbours. You know how he loves to frighten them." She said.

A short while later Jamie heard the sound of his Dad's car pulling up outside the house. Jamie got up and looked out of the bedroom window and down on to the drive. There, getting out of the passenger side of the car was his Grandad.

Jamie's Grandad was quite small with a withered crinkly face and thick bushy eyebrows, a scrawny neck, a slight body, thin gangly arms and hands with long bony fingers (of which one of them carried a crooked old walking stick) and the most amazing pair of thin bandy legs that anybody had ever seen in the whole wide world. But, not only that, this amazing little man was still wearing the same clothes that Jamie last saw him wearing. The red and black tartan kilt with matching thick woolly socks, a grey tweed jacket and also a silly, huge, great, hat, his 'Tam o Shanter.' His Grandad just stood there, with one hand clenched on his hip just looking at the house, eyeing every nook and cranny. He looked up at Jamie's window gave a huge smile and waved at Jamie. Jamie smiled and waved back. He flopped down onto his bed and thought to himself "These holidays are going to be fantastic. Look out neighbours there's a storm brewing and it's called McGregor."

A moment later, he heard his Mother calling him. "Jamie" called his Mum. "Come down your Grandads here." Jamie didn't reply, as he was lost in his own thoughts as to what the coming few weeks might bring. "Jamieee" called his Mum again (only louder this time)

"Coming" mumbled Jamie.

Jamie slowly stepped down the stairs and into the living room where he stopped. He was half expecting some trick or something from his Grandad as he was well known as a practical joker. "Ahh, here you are at last," said Jamie's Mum. Jamie came and just looked at the figure of his Grandad in front of him and said nothing. "At least say hello" said Jamie's father.

"Uh... Oh hello" said Jamie in a rather wary voice. His Grandad looked at him and then said in a broad Scottish accent. "Well come a wee bit closer laddee then I can have a better look at ye, Aye you've certainly grown a bit since aw last saw ye." Jamie walked over to his Granddad who leaned over towards him, and put his hands on Jamie's shoulders and looked very closely into Jamie's eyes. Jamie looked back into the old man's clear and sparkling grey eyes and there they both stood for a moment and neither spoke a word. Then the old man stood up straight again and still looking at Jamie said, "Aye, you're coming along fine." He then brought both his hands quickly over Jamie's ears and caught hold of them. "Left or Right" demanded Grandad. Jamie giggled and struggled to escape the clutch of his Grandad's bony hands then suddenly Jamie remembered the game. "Left...it's left," cried Jamie.

"Left ye say" replied Grandad.

"Yes, left," said Jamie.

"But... right feels better" Grandad replies.

"Ok right then" Jamie cried.

"Oh! Changing your mind now are ye," said Grandad.

"Yes!" said Jamie.

"So, what's it to be, LEFT or right?" questioned Grandad. With the emphasis firmly on the word left.

The game continued like this for a couple of minutes with Grandad changing the emphasis from left to right and Jamie changing his mind also until Grandad finally said "Ok! I want a final answer. Now which is it to be, Left or right?"

Jamie was just about to answer when Grandad interrupted him. "Just remember what I've always told you, always follow your instinct."

Jamie thought for a few seconds before replying "left"

Grandad then pulled his hands away from Jamie's ears and from Jamie's left ear produced a brand new shiny £1 coin. Grandad then held out his hand with the £1 coin still in it and offered it to Jamie. As Jamie went to take the offering Grandad's hand suddenly snapped shut. "Double or quits," said Grandad.

"OK!" said Jamie. Grandad did not move any of his hands but just stood there with the same hand as before held out with fist clenched and just looked at Jamie.

"OK, which hand?" asked Grandad. Jamie just looked at the only choice available. Grandad's left hand. It had not changed position since Grandad clamped it shut a moment since. The £1 coin must still be there. Jamie touched Grandad's clenched hand "That one", said Jamie.

"Are you sure?" said Grandad.

"Positive," replied Jamie.

"Are you absolutely sure?" asked Grandad.

"Yes! Jamie said.

"Are you absolutely sure that there is a £1 coin in that hand?" asked Grandad

"YES!" cried Jamie, with more than a hint of frustration in his voice.

"OK then" said Grandad and slowly opened his hand.

Jamie raised his hand to snatch his prize but stopped short as his eyes stared in disbelief at ... not a £1 coin but a brand new shiny £2 one. Jamie's parents and Grandad burst out laughing at the clever trick, and at the astonished look on Jamie's face which turned into a huge grin as he looked at his Grandad's laughing face.

Grandad rubbed Jamie's head as he placed the coin into Jamie's hand and said. "Here spend it wisely, and remember... very, very few things are what they appear to be."

Jamie thought about this for a few seconds turned to his parents "Can I go out to play?" he said.

"Yes, I suppose so," she laughed", only until your tea is ready," said Jamie's Mum. "Go on, off you go." Jamie scurried off to play. Dad and Grandad talked while his Mum prepared tea.

The next morning Jamie came down to breakfast and found his Grandad already up and dressed and tucking into a big bowl of thick steaming hot porridge. Jamie sat at his usual place at the table and watched his Grandad shovel great big spoonfuls of the stuff into his mouth. He watched as each spoonful created a huge lump in his Grandad's throat which was then gulped down his scrawny neck. Grandad suddenly stopped eating and turned his head towards Jamie, "What's better than a bowl o hot steaming porridge?" he asked.
Jamie looked back at Grandad "What?" replied Jamie who was a bit stunned by the suddenness of the question.
"What's better than, a bowl o porridge?" repeated Grandad.
"I don't know," said Jamie.
"Two bowls" said Grandad who then let out a cackle of laughter before carrying on with his shovelling and gulping. Jamie, his Mum, and his Dad just looked at each other until a slow grin crept across his Fathers face. Jamie just smiled and thought to himself that he must remember to watch out for Grandad's wierd sense of humour.

A short while later Jamie's Mum and Dad had to leave for work but not before they had a word with Jamie. "Now you will be a good boy, won't you?" said Jamie's Mum to him.
"Yes I will", said Jamie.
"Good" said Jamie's Mum. "Now we won't be gone long, see you later." Jamie watched from the window as his parents closed the door behind them, got into their car, and sped off.
Jamie turned away from the window and was heading back towards the kitchen when he heard the sound of a mobile phone going off to the tune of 'Scotland the Brave' then he heard his Grandad's voice "Allo...aye McGregor speaking...urgent meeting!... Serious business!... soon as

possible...aye ok...you'll have the co-ordinates then ... aye that's right...the public park...about fifteen minutes ...ok...bye" Jamie by this time had reached the kitchen entrance and was listening to Grandad's side of the conversation, more than a little intrigued by what he had seen and heard.

"Is that a new phone Grandad? Jamie asked.

Grandad didn't reply but was busy looking out of the window muttering and then looked at Jamie and then back at his phone. "Was it important?" Jamie asked. Grandad did not answer straight away but he turned to face Jamie. Finally, Grandad spoke. "It's very important." His face was set firm and his eyes were nearly closed through squinting. "I shall have to go", said Grandad, and at this Grandad walked out of the kitchen.

Grandad returned a moment later, he was wearing his jacket and his 'Tam' and carrying his walking stick "Right Laddie we're going on a wee trip."

"Where are we going?" asked Jamie.

"Don't know yet...we'll only find out when we get there," said Grandad.

"What do you mean?" Asked Jamie

"I mean exactly what I said," answered Grandad "I don't know where we are going yet."

"Is it a mystery tour?" Jamie asked.

"Well...it's a mystery to me," said Grandad "At least for the moment."

"You're being very secretive Grandad," said Jamie.

"I'm being honest. Come on we need to go," said Grandad The next thing Jamie knew, he was being 'marched' out of the house and along the street. Grandad was setting a fair pace and Jamie had to put a bit of a run on just to keep up. "Where are we going Grandad?" Jamie asked for the 'umpteenth' time in two minutes only to be told again that he'll find out when he gets there.

They walked along the high street until they came to a crossing. Grandad touched the button with the end of his walking stick and immediately the green crossing light came on. They crossed the busy road and walked through the entrance into the public park. They strode past the ranks of pretty flowers and on towards the bronze statue of a man sat upon a chair with one foot crossed over the other. The foot of the crossed leg had been rubbed, smooth, and shiny as it was a local tradition to give the shoe a quick rub as you passed by and it would bring you good luck. Grandad gave the shoe a very light tap with his stick as he passed and then stopped dead in his tracks and stared at Jamie, Jamie stared back.

"What?" Jamie said. Grandad didn't answer; he just raised his stick and pointed it at the statue. Jamie got the message and he walked back to the statue and jumped up to touch the shiny shoe of the statue. Satisfied at this Grandad then set off, again at great pace before turning left along a path, which led towards the duck pond. At the pond, Grandad ran his stick along the railing (which was there to prevent people from falling into the pond). It made a great clatter and made the few people who were nearby to glare disapprovingly at Grandad at which he took not the slightest, bit of notice. He then put his hand into his pocket and threw a handful of what Jamie could only guess was some kind of seed into the air and into the pond. The second that the seed hit the water there was an almighty commotion. The fish in the pond began to leap and jump and splash in the water to get at the seeds closely followed by squawking quacking ducks and honking geese, who came flying into the melee, feathers flying everywhere biting and squabbling at each other. Jamie looked at Grandad who had carried on walking at the same brisk pace and saw him give a little chuckle to himself.

They headed on up the path to the bandstand. They crossed the place where the public would sit and listen to any concerts that would be on and then through a line of trees into a large grassed open area. This is where Grandad stopped. He looked at his watch "Should be along any second now" he said. He had hardly stopped speaking when Jamie felt a strange sensation. There was a strong electric charge in the air. The hairs on his head stood straight up. There was stillness all around them. Jamie wanted to speak but was somehow scared of breaking the eerie silence, which seemed to envelope them. Then they were aware of a thick mist, which was coming down around them. Jamie clutched at Grandad's hand and hoped for some reassurance that all was well. Grandad just looked straight ahead and seemed completely unconcerned. "Don't be feared lad" said Grandad. Suddenly a big dark shadow appeared some metres above their heads and a few metres in front of them. It slowly descended in front of them and landed without the slightest sound. Jamie heard a sharp loud 'hiss' as though someone had opened a large bottle of fizzy lemonade. A door slid open and a set of steps came down and stopped at exactly the right spot in front of them. Grandad just had to reach out his foot to stand on the first one without moving left or right to get on board.

Jamie just gazed at the craft, which had just landed, he could just about make out its shape through the thick mist, which still surrounded the strange craft. It was about twenty metres long and had a round fuselage like a plane but it had no wings. There were flight fins coming out of the tail section. Along the side, there were round porthole type windows and the whole rocket ship gleamed, as though it was pure gold.

Jamie's Grandad stepped on board the craft without taking the slightest bit of notice of its shape, size, colour, or anything and disappeared inside. Jamie just stood there, mouth wide open trying to take it all in when his Grandad appeared in the doorway "Don't just stand there lad, get on board," said Grandad. Jamie gingerly stepped aboard the craft and made his way along the centre aisle. Alongside each side of him there where rows of red seats all facing towards the front except for one set in the middle which faced each other separated by a table. At the very front behind a white panel there was what appeared to be a cockpit where (Jamie supposed) was where the Pilot sat, with all the controls.

Jamie chose a seat on the left hand side of the rocket and moved across the seat until he was next to the window. During this time, Jamie's Grandad had been inside the driver's cockpit and was just walking out followed by the driver. He was a round jolly fellow who came up to Jamie and introduced himself "Tom, the bus, that's me, and I'm at your service young Sir" said the driver in a Welsh accent.

"I'm Jamie" Jamie replied.

"Pleased to meet you" said Tom.

"What is this thing? Is it a rocket ship? Is it yours?" Jamie asked.

Tom gave a little laugh "NOOO! It isn't mine" replied Tom (taking a seat beside Jamie) "but I do look after it and it takes up no end of my time. Why, only the other day, I spent hours, cleaning, and polishing and doing all manner of things. Why do you know?" Jamie's Grandad who very loudly cleared his throat cut Toms chattering abruptly short.

"We are in a hurry!" Grandad said.

"Oh! Yes... righto then ... I'll ... we'll ... get going then," stammered Tom. At this Tom got up and made his way back to the cockpit and the door slid quietly shut behind him. There was a low 'whirring' noise to the rear of the aircraft and Jamie turned to see the steps to board the aircraft fold themselves up and the door close behind them. Grandad sat down beside Jamie,

"Grandad" said Jamie. "Will you please, please, please tell me where we are going? And what is this thing?"

Grandad turned and looked at Jamie "Why, we're going to New York of course" replied Grandad.

"WHAT! BUT...WHY?" stammered Jamie.

Grandad put his hand into his pocket, and pulled out a paper bag and offered it to Jamie "sweet?"

Jamie looked at the bag that was offered, and then looked at the grin on Grandad's face. The look said it all. Jamie was not going to get any answers to his questions until Jamie had played the 'take a sweet before I say anything more game'. Jamie put his hand into the bag, and pulled out a sweet and popped it into his mouth. "Have another" said Grandad. "The red ones are really nice."

Jamie turned to look out the window but could not see much as the aircraft was still shrouded in thick fog, which seemed to cling on to the sides of it. Jamie thought that it was going to be a long and boring journey. However, a few moments after they took off the fog gradually disappeared and Jamie could now see clearly. They were high above the clouds in brilliant sunshine and judging by the rate at which the clouds were flying by they were travelling extremely fast. Faster than any normal aircraft in fact, thought Jamie. Jamie turned to his Grandad and said, "Right...now tell me just what is going on. Where are we going? Why are we going there and what is this thing we're flying in? Jamie had his really serious face on now and was really demanding answers to his questions.

Grandad glanced casually out of the window before turning back to Jamie. He too had his serious face on.

"Ok...we are going to New York. We are going there because something very serious has happened. Something so serious that a very extraordinary meeting has been called and I have been summoned to attend this meeting" Jamie was bursting with questions but he decided to keep calm as Jamie knew from past experience that to keep 'firing' questions at Grandad was unlikely to yield any truthful answers or indeed any kind of sensible answers at all.

"Ok! So, we're going to a meeting," said Jamie.

"Yes but not just any meeting. This is a meeting of the High Council. The High Council of I.H.C.I.U.P." said Grandad.

Jamie looked at Grandad for a few seconds before saying, "Grandad, I hope this is not one of your silly pranks, a very good one if it is and just what is hiccup?"

"No not hiccup but let me explain what it is. Grandad then went on to explain what the organisation was and what they do. Jamie listened intently without questioning and waited until Grandad had finished talking.

"Ok...so what has happened to call the meeting?" Jamie asked.

"Well"...began Grandad "I only had a brief talk with the head of the High Council but it seems we have a Dragon on the loose."

CHAPTER TWO

A Smooth/Bumpy Ride

"A Dragon...what exactly do you mean by a Dragon," asked Jamie.

"The normal type, you read about in myths and legends. You know all big and scaly with teeth and horns...oh and of course breathing fire" replied Grandad.

Jamie looked out of the window for a few seconds and then turned to Grandad.

"This is a wind up isn't it," he laughed. "You're having me on. Come on look me in the eye Grandad. I know this is a joke" Grandad turned to Jamie and looked him straight in the eye. They held each other's gaze for at least thirty seconds. Jamie was first to speak.

"You're serious...this is for real isn't it? Grandad just nodded then said, "welcome to my world Jamie."

Jamie turned and looked out of the window once more. There were a thousand things whirling around in his head and he could not think properly so he just looked at the clouds far below whizzing past. Jamie wondered exactly how fast they were going but the ride was so very smooth. There was no noise and no shaking. In fact if it wasn't for the fact that you could see through the windows and watch the clouds flash past you that you knew that you were moving at all. He turned and asked his Grandad. "How fast are we going?"

"Oh I don't know son, I never bother with all that technical nonsense" said his Grandad "yon daft pilot may tell ye," he added.

"Can I go and ask him?" Jamie said.

"Aye I suppose so." Grandad said. Jamie jumped up from his seat, and ran along the aisle and up to the cockpit and politely knocked on the door.

There was a low 'hiss' as the door almost immediately slid aside, Tom was sat in the only seat in the cockpit. It was right in the middle of the cockpit and he turned to see who was coming into the cabin.

"Hello there" he said to Jamie giving a big jolly smile as he said so. "Come to see me have you? Well come in don't be shy," Jamie stepped into the cabin. He expected to see lots of instruments and things but was surprised to find none at all. There was a big window in front of him and Jamie could see all the clouds below which began to disappear and he could see the sea far below sparkling every now and then. "Wow this is great!" said Jamie. "Where are we?"

"Over the sea" Tom said, grinning.

"I can see that" Jamie said. "But which sea and where exactly are we?"

"We are over the Atlantic and we are ten blips from where we are going."

"Ten blips, what's a blip?" said Jamie.

"A blip is like a mach, only faster," said Tom.

"What's a mach?" asked Jamie.

"Mach is the speed of sound" Tom replied. "But a Blip is a lot faster than a mach." Tom then added. Jamie thought for a second then decided that perhaps he should now change the question away from 'blips'.

"How do you make it fly?" He asked, looking blankly at the lack of controls.

"Oh you don't fly it," replied Tom, "you ride it."

"What do you mean?" Jamie asked.

"This is not flying," Tom replied again. "This is more like a bus than a plane and she rides the wave's man." At this last sentence Tom took up the stance of a surfer with his arms held out wide and his legs standing sideways, his body in a crouch as though balancing on a surf board.

"I don't understand," Jamie said.

"Oh! It's quite simple." Tom said. "This aircraft is not an aeroplane. It does not fly."

Jamie looked puzzled. "Can you explain a bit more?"

"Well" said Tom, "this aircraft is what we call an 'AGR 04'. This stands for Aircraft, Gravity Reflecting Mark 4."

"How does it work?" asked Jamie.

"Well" replied Tom. "You know that a mirror reflects light?" Jamie nodded "Well, imagine a mirror that reflects gravity. This aircraft can reflect back the Earth's gravity and uses the Earth's magnetic field to get from one place to the other very quickly. We call them 'Gravity Reflectors'. This means that this ship can deflect Earth's gravity thus causing a gravity wave we then ride this wave and guide it to where we want it to go. Simple."

"But there are no buttons or switches, there are no controls" said Jamie

"Ah!" replied Tom, "watch" Tom swung round and picked up a set of headphones, which were hanging on the wall behind him. He placed them over his head and flicked a small switch on the right of the headset. There was a small microphone attached to the headset and Tom adjusted it to his mouth. "Computer, display flight controls," Tom said into the microphone. A split second later the whole panel (which previously had been just blank and opaque) lit up with a whole set of instruments showing everything from altitude and speed to time and temperature.

Jamie looked at the dazzling array that had appeared before him. "Wow, this is really cool" Jamie said. Tom then began to explain what each and every control did and he explained that during normal travel they did not usually have the flight controls on view because the computer controls the whole aircraft and once the destination has been programmed in, the computer takes over and deals with all the aircrafts controls and functions.

"Can you fly it manually?" asked Jamie.

"Yes we can" Tom replied. "Would you like to see?"

"Yes please" Jamie answered.

"OK, stand back a bit." Tom said. Jamie stood back as Tom spoke into his headset microphone once again, "Computer, set deck for manual flight, configuration Tom 023." There came a bleeping noise from the panel shortly followed by some flashing lights and then suddenly to Jamie's astonishment the whole flight deck changed shape... The front of the panel slid back a little and the sides came around to form a semi circular shape around the pilot's seat. A panel opened up near Tom's feet, and up slid a control column with a small semi circular steering wheel and on the floor appeared some foot pedals.

Jamie was very impressed. "It looks very complicated." Jamie said.

"Piece of cake, just watch this" Tom took hold of the control column and spoke into his headset microphone. "Computer, change to manual control, Tom 023." There was a slight pause before a woman's voice spoke up from the flight deck.

"WARNING! BECAUSE OF AIR SPEED AND TURBULENCE. CHANGING TO MANUAL CONTROL WILL AFFECT THIS AIRCRAFTS STABILITY"

Tom immediately replied "Oh! Be quiet, a bit of turbulence never hurt anyone. Computer, warning acknowledged, change to manual control, Tom 023."

There was a slight pause before suddenly the aircraft began to shudder and shake violently and Jamie had to grab hold of the back of Tom's seat as he was 'thrown' from side to side. Tom was 'whooping' and yelling as the aircraft was 'tossed' here and there as he wrestling with the controls. The aircraft suddenly lurched upwards before the nose of the aircraft dived down very steeply. They flashed through some thick clouds with the aircraft shuddering more violently. They carried on going through the cloud, still diving down for what Jamie thought went on for ages before they suddenly broke out of it and there in front of them, filling the whole of the windscreen was the ocean, which was getting closer by the second.

Jamie could now see the white tops of the waves as they hurtled downwards and he could feel a scream welling up in his throat as he clung on to the back of Tom's seat, his fingernails were white as they bit into the soft padding. Jamie closed his eyes and his arms stiffened as he tried to brace himself for the impact. A scream was just about to burst from Jamie's lips when

Tom suddenly heaved on the control column. The aircraft responded immediately and it levelled out just a couple of metres above the water. Tom let out a scream of delight as he turned around to face Jamie. "Would you like to have a go? Tom asked.

Jamie did not reply. He was still clinging on to the seat with his eyes still shut. He slowly opened them. "What happened, are we ok?" He said.

"Of course we are" replied Tom. "Great fun wasn't it?"

"No it wasn't" came a reply from the back of them. It was Grandad. He was not at all amused. "Jamie, get back in here." He ordered. Jamie obeyed. Grandad turned to follow Jamie but paused in the doorway. He turned his head slightly toward Tom "Get this thing back on its flight path before someone spots us and no more messing about...oh! And, by the way, I'll see you later" he said sternly.

When they got back in their seats, Jamie turned to his Grandad and said. "It wasn't Tom's Fault that we were messing about Grandad, I asked Tom to show me how it works."

"It's alright son." Grandad said. "I'll not be too hard on the lad. But, you must realise that we are on serious business, I know I should not have brought you along with me, but I had no choice, I could not have left you all alone in the house."

"What sort of business is it all about?" asked Jamie.

"Well." Began Grandad, "as I told you before, I believe that a serious incident has occurred that involves Grimfell."

"Who or what is Grimfell?" asked Jamie.

You're not listening properly are you?" said Grandad.

"I am, I am protested Jamie. Grandad looked at Jamie and thought for a few seconds before saying. "Ok" Grandad said. "Grimfell is a Dragon. In fact, he is the last of the great Royal land Dragons. He has been held captive in China for the last twelve hundred years but now he has escaped. The great beastie is out and about and who knows what calamity he may cause."

"Ok" said Jamie "and what about the High Council?"

"The High Council" began Grandad "is a very ancient society. It was set up centuries ago to protect the world from strange and evil forces. It is a group drawn together from all over the world. These people are possessed with great knowledge and wisdom who have been appointed to investigate strange goings on and to make sure that no real harm comes to anyone."

"Like the police?" Jamie asked.

"Yes," said Grandad.

"But you don't look like a policeman Grandad...Or someone with great knowledge and wisdom" said Jamie

Grandad gave Jamie a wry smile.

"Aye well, that's the whole point of it. You see son sometimes it doesn't pay to advertise, understand what I'm saying?" said Grandad. Jamie just looked at him and shook his head. "Well, we're like secret agents all our work, is done in secret. We tell no one and we involve no one except ourselves, and if no one see's us or hears of us as we carry out our business then our job is well done. However, there have been occasions when we have had to use the press and television to make up stories that keep our work secret."

Jamie pondered this for a moment before asking "Is your work dangerous and what did you mean by evil?" asked Jamie. And why don't you just tell the police or the Army so that they can deal with it?"

"Aye well, they can't deal with things they don't understand." Grandad said. "A wise man once said *'There are more things between heaven and earth than are dreamed of in your philosophy Horatio'* Grandad turned and looked deep into Jamie eyes and spoke in a very low voice.

"I have seen things that you will never see, some wonderful and amazing, fantastic things. I have also seen some horrible, nasty, terrible evil things that would make your blood freeze, your bones crack and your skin crawl, things that would turn your brain into a sponge and turn you into a gibbering lunatic." A small shiver went down Jamie's spine as Jamie looked directly into Grandad's eyes. Gone was the smile. Gone was any sign of mirth or laughter that Jamie was used to seeing in his Grandad's kindly face Jamie realised that Grandad was being deadly serious.

A few seconds passed before Grandad spoke again, "but, don't you worry young man." Grandad's voice now came back to normal. "I'll always be here to protect ye from all the baddies."

Jamie turned and looked out of the window "look Grandad, I can see some land down there"

Grandad looked. "Aye, we'll be landing soon." He said.

"Will we be using an airport?" Jamie asked.

"Nope" said Grandad and shook his head.

"Will we be using a park to land in then?" asked Jamie.

"Nope" said Grandad and again shook his head

"Where then" asked Jamie.

"We'll probably land on someone's roof. Just like Father Christmas," replied Grandad.

Jamie just gave Grandad a funny look and said "Oh yes, which one"

"The one with a big flashing sign on the roof saying 'Land here' and an arrow pointing to the spot." Jamie thought that Grandad was just being silly and carried on looking out of the window. The aircraft was slowing down now and was getting lower and lower.

After a few seconds Jamie could see that they were flying above a big city, and as the aircraft got lower, Jamie could make out a big tall square building with a flat roof and on the roof Jamie could see a big flashing sign Saying 'LAND HERE' and there was also a big arrow pointing to a circle. "Told you so," said Grandad grinning at Jamie. Jamie didn't say anything in reply but he did blush slightly.

CHAPTER THREE

CLOUD BASE

The aircraft touched down without the slightest bump, the door slid open and the steps stretched out and on to the roof of the building. "Come on son" said Grandad to Jamie as he led Jamie down the aisle of the rocket and then out on to the roof of the building. They walked along the roof towards a door, which was part of a little square building placed in one of the corners. There was a big stern looking Policeman at the entrance and above the door was the letters I.H.C.I.U.P.

The Policeman stood to attention, saluted smartly, and opened the door for them. They went through the door and into a hallway, which contained a lift. The lift doors were open and Jamie followed Grandad into the lift. Inside the lift was a man who was dressed like a hotel porter, complete with uniform. He smiled at Jamie and his Grandad and with an American accent said, "Good morning Sir's, going up?" Grandad nodded and the porter turned around to a row of buttons sited on the wall and pushed a button marked 'UP'. Jamie was just about to say to Grandad that we are already at the top of the building and can't possibly go up any higher when Jamie felt the lift takeoff. Jamie could just see through a small rectangular window in the lift door that they were indeed going upwards as they passed through a small cloud on their way up.

The journey lasted only a few seconds though and Jamie felt the lift come to a stop, a bell went 'Ding' and the doors opened. To Jamie's amazement they were inside a building. Grandad left the lift and stepped into a wide entrance hall. Jamie followed him and then stopped to look at the sight which fell before him.

The entrance hall was made of beautiful marble walls with tall pillars that held up a pale blue sky with clouds that actually looked like real clouds. Jamie looked again at the clouds. They were moving. They were real clouds and it was real sky. Jamie just stood opened mouthed. He heard his Grandad calling him from behind and Jamie answered "coming" but continued to look upwards and at the same time walking backwards. Suddenly Jamie tripped over something and tumbled backwards and landed onto a three metre, square platform, which was located approximately in the middle of the reception area.

Jamie looked around to see what it was that he had fallen onto when he let out a terrifying scream. There before Jamie's eyes was ... nothing. Nothing except the roof of the building which they landed on a moment or two ago, only it was hundreds of feet below them. The patch of floor that Jamie had landed on was invisible, he could feel a solid hard floor, but he couldn't see it, which was very frightening.

Jamie felt someone's hands around his waist, picked him up and put him back on his feet on solid normal flooring. "You Ok kid?" said a voice. It belonged to the man who had brought them up in the lift. Jamie just nodded and was still looking down trying to work out what was happening. Jamie was trying to work out what kind of building this was? What was holding the building up? What was the see-through floor made of? Jamie could feel a real, hard, solid floor. It was all very confusing for him.

"Welcome to Cloud base, first visit uh kid?" The lift- man asked smiling at him. "Don't worry you'll get used to it."

"But how do you know that there's a floor there to be walked on and not just a hole in the floor?" asked Jamie.

"It's formed by Hard Light." It was Grandad, he came back when he heard Jamie cry out. "And don't worry about falling you'll never feel a thing if you fell all the way down there" he said smiling.

"What's hard light?" asked Jamie. Grandad thought for a moment before clearing his throat saying.

"It's complicated."

"You don't know." Jamie replied.

"Yes I do." Grandad said.

"Well what is it then?" asked Jamie.

"What do they teach you at school?" asked Grandad.

"Nothing about Hard Light." replied Jamie.

"What! Not even in physics?" cried Grandad in mock alarm.

"You know they don't," replied Jamie.

Grandad grinned. "You know science is not my strongpoint," he said.

"I thought that you wouldn't know" Jamie said. Grandad walked on towards the reception area closely followed by Jamie. Grandad then stopped, turned to Jamie, and said, "Ice."

"Pardon?" said Jamie.

"Hard Light is like ice." Grandad said.

"How?" asked Jamie.

"Well..." Began Grandad. "When water freezes it changes from a liquid into a solid, is that not so?" asked Grandad.

"Yes" Jamie answered.

"Then it's the same for light" exclaimed Grandad. "Except that you don't freeze light you just need to change its molecular structure and then beam it across a special frame and Hey Presto! You have a hard light chamber...easy."

"But how do you change..." Grandad stopped Jamie dead in his next question by putting his hand across Jamie's mouth. "Here endeth the science lesson." Grandad said.

They then they turned into a corridor. There were no more 'holes' to fall into here. The floor here was now solid and this made Jamie feel a lot safer. There were several doors leading off both left and right which they walked straight passed until they came to the end of the corridor where, there was a double door, which had a sign saying

'SPECIAL COUNCIL MEMBERS ONLY. VISITORS PLEASE SIGN IN AT THE DESK.'

Before the doors there was a desk, which had a Policeman seated at it. They stopped at the desk Grandad, was asked to 'Sign in' by the Policeman and Grandad did so. "What about the young man" the Policeman said to Grandad.

"He's with me." Grandad said.

"Then you'll have to sign for him too sir." said the Policeman, and pointed to a sign, which said:

> *All non-members must, be signed for and sworn in. All non-members, must be accompanied into the chambers and stay accompanied throughout the debate. All non-members are to remain the responsibility of the accompanied member who shall ensure that the non-member shall conduct himself or herself properly at all times in a manner befitting the occasion. All non-members, who don't conduct themselves accordingly will be asked to remove themselves from the chamber and will take no further part in the debate...*

The list of rules governing none members went on and on. Grandad looked at the sign with a frown on his face then gave out a sigh and said. "I can guess who wrote that load o nonsense! Just give me the paper here I'll sign the daft thing." The Policeman handed over a copy of the declaration and a pen, which Grandad signed and handed back. "Right son, come on" said Grandad to Jamie and was about to walk through the double doors when the Policeman said.

"Just a minute Sir, we haven't finished yet" and at that he pinned on Jamie's jumper a small plastic card with the word 'Visitor' emblazoned on it. He now asked Jamie to stand against the wall where his photograph was taken. Grandad looked the policeman, shook his head, and said. "More rubbish" He then asked the Policeman. "Is that it now?"

"Yes Sir, that's it." The Policeman answered and with that, Grandad put his hand on Jamie's shoulder and both went through the double doors.

They entered a large room with a high vaulted ceiling, oak panelled walls, and a large oval table in the middle. Around the table were seated twelve elderly people from different parts of the world judging by the differing dress and colours of the people who all looked at the new comers.

The man at the head of the table spoke. "Ah Mr McGregor you're here at last and with a visitor too I see."

"I came as fast as I could" answered Grandad and as he did so he led Jamie to a chair which was standing next to a small table in a corner of the room. Grandad seemed to know most of the other people especially the big American who he sat next to. Grandad turned to Jamie. "You just sit there and be quiet and I'll try and get this over as quick as I can," whispered Grandad. Grandad then took his place at the big table with the rest of the elderly men. "Sorry I had to bring the kid along but I'm supposed to be babysitting," said Grandad, now addressing the rest of the room. There were a few sniggers of laughter and the odd comment which was jokingly said among the people in the room. Jamie felt very indignant, "I'm not a baby," thought Jamie who sat there, his arms crossed and his feet swinging and feeling quite 'miffed'.

The man at the head of the table got up to speak, "Right then, I think we're all here now so we can proceed with the meeting" The man who spoke was quite small and round with a ruddy complexion and had a thick 'Yorkshire' accent which seemed inappropriate somehow given the surroundings. "I will now call the meeting to order," he said and as he said so he banged a small wooden hammer on the table. "Today is the twentieth day of July. Present at this extraordinary meeting are the esteemed Mr Liu Chung, The Esteemed Mrs Bhattacharya. The Esteemed ... The proceedings were interrupted by Jamie's Grandad who stood up and said, "Can we just get on with it. Instead of all this blather?"

The Chairman stood up and said, "Now! Now! Mr McGregor, tha's owt of order, we have a certain protocol, which has, to be followed as laid down in the statute of 1778, which states (and I quote) "That at meetings of the Security Council it is the responsibility of the Chairman, (That being me) to ensure that full and appropriate acknowledgements are duly carried out and that ...."

Again Jamie's Grandad interrupted him "We're wasting time Man. Let's get on with the real business of why we're here. We all know who we are."

Again the Chairman tried to shut Grandad up. "If you don't stop interrupting, McGregor I'll serve a motion of censure on you, as laid down in the 'Powers of Chairmanship Act of Seventeen sixty two paragraphs three subsection two..." Again Jamie's Grandad interrupted him,

"Sit down you old 'windbag' afore I.".....said Grandad waving his stick in the air in a threatening manner.

"Oh! threatening behaviour now is it" said The Chairman, "well let me tell you, that under the special powers granted to me by the Security Council Act of ..." (The rest of what the Chairman said was lost in the noise that followed) everyone was trying to talk at once, people stood up with fingers pointing and arms waving. Finally, order was restored when the Chairman started to hit the table with his wooden hammer and was shouting. "Order, Order." Everyone sat down and calm, was restored. "Right lets have no more of that nonsense, I'll continue ... note in the minutes, meeting disrupted by J. R. McGregor who's constant interruptions have resulted in ..." again Grandad jumped up before the chairman could finish

"What the 'eck' are you on about now man?" Grandad Shouted. He had to be restrained by others as he tried to get to the Chairman. The Chairman was upon his feet now and pointing his finger and quoting more rules and regulations at Grandad. Chaos ensued as others joined in and very soon, they were all at it again, arguing and shouting at each other.

Jamie sat for a while and could not believe the sight before him, grown men and women behaving like children. He put his hands over his ears to try and shut out the noise but it was no use. He tried closing his eyes but it still did not work. Jamie was beginning to become very annoyed when a very clear calming voice which stopped all the bickering. The voice came from the lovely Indian woman, Mrs Bhattacharya. "We have to stop behaving like this, we are not setting a very good example to our guest, I suggest that we all sit down and discuss this like 'grown up' people."

Jamie felt enchanted by her soft silky voice. There was just a trace of an accent as she spoke and it felt as if the whole world stopped to listen to her. "There is a need to progress the meeting Mr Chairman" continued Mrs Bhattacharya "I suggest that we move straight to the point of the meeting."

"Right to business then" said the Chairman. "It has come to light that there has been a development with regard to the safe incarceration of the Dragon 'Grimfell' The Esteemed Liu Chung. May the ..." (The chairman started to give acknowledgements then thought better of it) "will now proceed with the details." All eyes now looked upon Liu Chung.

Liu Chung was Chinese, quite small and slim with sharp facial features. He wore a moustache, which grew from the sides of his top lip down under his chin where both ends were then, braided together to a small beard which then hung down about 10 centimetres and ended with a tiny black bow. He had long dark hair, which he had brushed to the back of his head and was now, plaited into a tight long 'Pony-tail, which went right down his back to his waist. He wore a long black leather coat, which fell below his knees. It was fastened, from the neck to the waist by a single row of nine buttons. The coat then flared out over his hips and Jamie thought that he looked quite sinister. Liu Chung began "As you know, because of the knowledge that my people had in the ways and habits of Lungs or Dragons as you may call them, it fell to us that we should be the keepers of the last remaining Dragon, Grimfell. Because of his powers and his tricky and treacherous nature, it was decided long ago that the beast should never be free to trouble and carry out chaos and mayhem to the people of the world again. We have carried out our duty for hundreds of years and although the task was wearisome, we have always carried out our duty. Until, recently that is. It is with deep regret that I have to inform the Council that we have failed in our duty and that Grimfell has escaped and is now free."

There was a loud gasp from the rest of the people around the table and everyone began talking at once. The Chairman banged the table and this brought silence to the debate. "Please, give order now" said the Chairman and asked Liu Chung to continue.

"In the beginning, our training of guards for the task to keep the Dragon passive was very good. Each guard was trained in the ways of how not to fall under his spell and in this way the Dragon could be controlled. However, it must be said that our training of guards in recent times must not have been very good because Grimfell has managed to put his spell upon his guards and they have allowed him to escape."

Again there were mutterings around the table and again the Chairman had to bring the meeting to order. Liu Chung spoke again. As he did so he got up and walked over to a map of the world which hung on the wall, "The last sighting we had was that he was heading south-east towards Japan."

At this point another man spoke from around the table. He was from Japan. He had similar features to Liu Chung only rounder. He was thicker in build with no facial hair or 'pony tail'. He did have a full head of hair but it was now a silver grey colour and cut in a familiar 'western' style and he wore a light grey suit with a collar and tie. "The Dragon was indeed headed for Japan," he said. "Not only heading, but got there. He reached Tokyo, smashed his way into the Tokyo museums archaeology department, and stole a particular artefact which had been found recently and shot off again, heading west."

Again there was a great and excited discussion among those who were around the table. The commotion was short lived as Mr Higginbottom banged his wooden hammer on the table. "Order!, Order! Give order now."

The Japanese man (whose, name Jamie found out later was Mr Yamamoto) now continued. "The artefact was found during an archaeological dig on Mount Fujiyama." There were then some questions from the other people about what the artefact was and it was some time before he got the chance to answer because everyone kept talking at once and interrupting when he tried to speak. It took Mr Higginbottom and his wooden hammer to shut everyone up again. Mr Yamamoto then gave a description of the item that the dragon stole. "The item was roughly egg shaped, about the size of a small rugby ball and appeared to be made of a solid, hard, 'glass-like' material which looked like amber but you could not see all the way to the centre."

There then followed a long and loud discussion about what the item could be. Someone asked a question about where the dragon could be now and everyone shook their heads. Then Mr Yamamoto spoke, "We don't know where he is going ...all we know is that he headed west." There was silence for a few seconds before Mr Liu Chung spoke again. "The dragon was headed West you say?" Mr Liu Chung pondered this question as he stroked his chin. "A map please," he then said.

Mr Higginbottom left his seat and walked over to the left side of the room near to the door, and flicked a switch. There was a feint 'whirring' noise as a screen lowered itself down from the ceiling very near the wall. He then produced a remote control and pushed a button. The screen lit up and a 'menu' appeared along the left hand side of the screen. Mr Higginbottom then used the remote control to 'scroll' down the menu until he highlighted the word 'Maps'. There he stopped and jabbed his finger on the keypad a further menu came up giving different countries and regions. "Which region?" asked Mr Higginbottom "Global" replied Liu Chung and then made his way towards the screen. Liu Chung stood before the screen which by now was showing the whole of the planet before him and began to trace a path with his finger from China down to Japan and then went west across Russia, Eastern Europe, Western Europe until he came to a place in Western Europe and stopped. "Here" said Liu Chung tapping his finger against the screen. "This is where he is heading." There were several cries of "Where?" Before Liu Chung spoke "His old Fortress of Bad Habitzberg." There was a deathly silence all around the room as he finished speaking.

The silence only lasted for a few seconds before everybody spoke at once. There was a clamour as everyone was shouting all at once before once again Mr Higginbottom brought the room to order and asked. "Mr McGregor you don't think that this has anything to do with your friend 'The Professor.' (This was a reference to Grandad's ex colleague and close friend Professor Helsingborg. They worked closely for years on certain projects until Helsingborg turned greedy, rejected the ideals of I.H.C.I.U.P. and is now in hiding and is a wanted man having stolen lots of secrets from the organisation.) Grandad looked up his eyes narrowing and then thought for a few seconds... "No! Dragons are not Helsingborg's style. He lacks the expertise. Technology is his thing. Machines and Science he understands. Mythological creatures don't compute with him."

"Right first things first, we need to warn the 'Authorities in that region to evacuate all the people. Put out the usual scare story a 'Plague' or a 'Rogue Satellite' is going to hit the area High risk of damage and radioactive material. That usually does the trick. Volunteers please to do the scary story." The Chairman said. Two or three hands went up. "OK go to it please." The people whose hands went up scurried out of the room.

Grandad was the first to speak up after the door closed "Ah suppose we've been lucky then that he's only taken a piece o rock so far, and we'll just have tae put him back in his pen again."

The Chairman spoke again "OK! Any suggestions as to how the deed is to be done?" Before anyone could answer, Mr Yamamoto spoke up.

"There is something else that I think that you should know." He paused before continuing. "The stone is not just a piece of rock. It is a very special stone. With very special properties."

"What kind of special properties?" asked Mr Higginbottom?

Mr Yamamoto hesitated before he answered. "It's very hard to explain," he stammered.

"Please try" asked Mrs Bhattacharya in a very soothing voice.

"Well" continued Mr Yamamoto. "The stone has a presence." There were some mutterings from around the table but they stopped when Mr Yamamoto started to talk again. "It glows an incandescent light when it's held and some of our people believe that it has spoken with them."

"A talking stone?" exclaimed Grandad. "Curioser and Curioser."

"Please," replied Mr Yamamoto "you do not understand. The stone does not really speak... it seems to... go inside your mind and finds out things. It's very strange."

This caused lots of excitement around the room and the chattering grew louder and louder.

The Chairman (Mr Higginbottom) banged his hammer again and brought the clamour to a halt. "Delegates" he said. "The task just became harder. Not only are we tasked to return the Dragon to his cage, but... it seems to me that also we should endeavour to return the stone intact to be studied."

"So why did the dragon steal the stone?" asked Grandad.

No one in the room could answer the question although several people tried but they were all dismissed. A debate ensued about the possible reasons why Grimfell would want the stone.

Mr Liu Chung now spoke up, "In China the Dragon is considered to be the wisest of creatures. For centuries Dragons would be honoured guests of all the emperors who would seek advice from them. Until, that is, one very foolish emperor decided that he would try and be as wise as the dragons by killing one and eating its brain. This started a great war and many men and dragons were slaughtered, thus began the Dragons demise because they were never as plentiful as men were, Grimfell must have sensed the finding of the stone. He must have known about the stone all along and when the opportunity presented itself, he escaped and went straight to it."

Mr Liu Chung stood up "We must get the stone back. This stone must be very important. The lives of a lot, of people may be at risk if we do not."

This gave rise to lots of nodding heads and "here here's" from the rest of the delegates. "The only thing is how it is to be done and quickly, before the Dragon can use the stone...for what... ever its use is," said the Chairman.

The man from the USA stood up to speak. His name was Rufus T. Cody. He was a big man from Texas who wore a big cowboy hat, cowboy boots, and who, also wore a thick handlebar moustache. He spoke in a slow southern drawl.

"If it be fittin Mr Chairman. I'd like to volunteer to lead a military force to go in thar and teach that Son of a" ... at this point the cowboy stopped talking as he could see that there were women present "Oh begging your pardon Ma'am" he said. "Now then where was I ... Oh yes. Why I reckon that with a detachment of Marines backed up with Infantry units from the 101st Airborne Battalion we could have that stone right back where it belongs in no time at all."

This started yet another furious row among those present until it eventually calmed down. The Chairman spoke. "How long would it take to organise such a force?" He asked. "Well let's see now.," said Rufus "Got to get the permission of the President, then there's Congress to pass a bill allowing this, Generals to brief, stores and transport to organise. Why I reckon it should take no more than a few weeks to get things moving." A collective groan went around the table. "Why, what's the matter?" said Rufus.

"We don't have a few weeks laddie," said Grandad. "A few days at the most, but certainly not weeks."

Mrs Bhattacharya now spoke. "I am not an expert in the ways of Dragons however, is there also the possibility that such a force would not be effective against Grimfell even if it was assembled against him today."

"You are right," said Mr Liu Chung "The fortress of Bad Habitzberg is deep in the Black Mountains and although I have never been there, I believe it to be almost impossible to break into. A Dragon such as Grimfell could hold off even the most determined Army for weeks if not months."

Jamie all this time had been listening intently to all that was said but remained quiet on his seat in the corner of the room. So intensely had Jamie been listening that he was leaning forward on his chair to hear more closely. He leaned over so far that suddenly the chair slipped from underneath him and Jamie went tumbling across the floor and landed in a big heap near his Grandad.

"What the..." Grandad said as he bent over to pick Jamie up "Why I'd forgotten all about ye son. Are ye alright?"

Jamie nodded and answered, "Yes, I'm OK"

"Perhaps I should take you out of here to somewhere where you'll be more comfortable." Grandad's eyebrows suddenly shot up and he had a big gleam in his eyes. "That's it," he exclaimed to the rest of the people gathered.

"What is?" Rufus said.

"Stealth Mon, that's what's required for this, plenty o stealth." He then turned around to Jamie "Well done son! I knew you would come in handy."

The Chairman now spoke up, "Could the Esteemed Mr McGregor kindly enlighten us as to what exactly he means by that?"

"Simple" said Grandad. "Jamie here has just given me an idea. You see, by keeping quiet everybody in the room had forgotten about him. (Until he fell over) Likewise I believe that a small band of determined and expertly trained people could perhaps 'sneak' into yon Fortress and 'whick the stone away from the Great Beastie afore he knows it and deliver it back into safe keeping thus leaving us plenty o time to deal with the monster later."

"But the whole reason we are here is to deal with the Dragon not the stone. We don't know what the stone is," said Liu Chung.

"That's true," said Grandad. "But the Dragon thinks it's very important to risk its neck to steal it. So let us make getting the stone back our priority. Because if we secure the stone. Then we could use it to entice the dragon back into his cage."

The room was silent for a few seconds then Rufus T Cody spoke. "You know what Mac; you just might have something there." The room now erupted into excited chatter with huge grins appearing on faces where only a short time before there was despair. The Chairman began to bang his hammer again and the excitement died down "Delegates" he said. "Is anyone opposed to the motion as forwarded by the Esteemed Mr McGregor?" There was no answer from anyone. "Right then, all those in favour of the motion please raise your hand." Everyone raised a hand. "Motion carried unanimously." The Chairman said. "Now then," he then said, "it's time to put some meat on the bone."

Explain please" said Liu Chung.

"Well, what I mean is." Said the Chairman, "just exactly who is this 'small band of men' going to comprise of and it needs to be done very, very quickly."

There was a moments silence before Liu Chung spoke, "I should like to offer my services to go to the Dragons lair and take back the stone." Everyone looked at Liu Chung as he said it. His head was bowed as he spoke "It is the very least I can do to help to repay the great danger that we have let loose on the world."

The Chairman said, "Well done lad, we are proud of you. Although I did not like to 'volunteer' on your behalf, but your expertise in the ways of Dragons will come in very handy to the team. Has anyone got anymore suggestions?" Again there was deathly silence, until Grandad said "I'll go with ye son, I'm no expert in the ways o Dragons. But I cannot let ye go by yourself to face yon terrible monster."

Liu Chung smiled at Grandad and said "Thank you. You are most welcome."

"I will go also," said Mr Yamamoto.

"You can put my name down too for that trip," Said Rufus T Cody, "I never could resist a good fight."

Mrs Bhattacharya now exclaimed. "I shall come along too, it might be rather exciting, and I haven't done anything exciting for a long time." The Chairman then said, "But it could be very dangerous, you could get into serious trouble. I cannot allow you to go."

Mrs Bhattacharya turned and looked at the Chairman and said, "You cannot stop me, besides, I may have some skills which the team could use. I am no stranger to mountains because I grew up in the Himalayas and I do possess knowledge of medicine. I am a Doctor you know."

Before the Chairman could reply Grandad said "Ye'll do fer me Lassie." and before the Chairman new it the 'small band' had grown to five. All the delegates were chattering away like excited, school boys amongst themselves and more volunteers were clammering to 'join up' and the Chairman had to bring the proceedings to order by (yet again) banging his hammer on the table. "Esteemed people," he said. "We cannot all go on this journey. If this 'expedition' is to succeed, it will indeed, (as Mr McGregor has already stated) rely on stealth. That means taking as few people as possible, using skills and techniques, which not all of you possess and I may add stealing back the 'Stone'. Now I appreciate that you are all mad keen to 'do your bit' but such matters as breaking into dragons lairs and stealing from them is best left to those who know about such things. Now, I'm not at all convinced that we have the necessary expertise to go about such business, but time is of the essence and the smaller the team then the better the chances of success. I propose that the five 'Esteemed' members who have bravely volunteered their services should be the only ones to go on the expedition. As for the rest of you I can assure you that you will be plenty busy during the next few days."

"Right that's settled, there's five of you. You are to leave today for the Black Mountains. The expeditionary force will meet in my office in ten minutes. We will need to discuss the best travel arrangements. Take whatever you think you may need for your journey, the rest of you will form the rear party and give all necessary support that is possible, Gods speed" and with that the Chairman banged down his hammer and said, "the meeting has ended." The meeting broke up with much hand shaking, back patting, and chattering among the delegates.

Jamie still sat there quite bemused by all the proceedings until his Grandad walked over to him.

"Well son," he said, "I told ye that there's seeerrious business afoot. Now then, what the 'eck' are we going to do with you?" Grandad just stood there rubbing his bony chin and eyeing up Jamie.

"Why, where are you going?" said Jamie. Grandad looked back in surprise.

"Have ye not been listening to a word that's been said?" Jamie thought for a second and then said. "Do you mean all that about Dragons and stuff?" Grandad put his hands on his hips and stared at Jamie for a second, and then said.

"Of course I mean all that about Dragons and 'stuff' what else would I mean?" Jamie looked down at his feet.

"Can I come too? I've always wanted to see a real live Dragon."

"Definitely not it's far too dangerous for a wee boy," said Grandad.

"Grandad, I'm as tall as you now, so I'm not such a wee boy am I? So what am I going to do?" said Jamie "will I have to go home?"

"Well" ... said Grandad "I'll have to see what I can arrange, come on." And with that he took Jamie's hand and led him out of the meeting room and back along the corridor and then out into the reception area. They walked over to the main desk and Grandad said something to a man who was behind it. The man nodded and picked up the handset of a phone which was lying on the desk, punched the keypad a few times, and then after a couple of seconds spoke to someone on the other end of the line. He then replaced the handset and Jamie heard him say, "He'll be along very shortly Sir."

"That's fine," replied Grandad.

Jamie amused himself by looking down through the 'Hard light' floor and looking at the tops of the buildings and all about the surrounding city. It was a marvellous sight. He then heard footsteps approaching and they stopped when they got to the desk. He heard Grandad talking to the man and then he heard the man say "sure, no problem sir. Is this the little guy?" Jamie looked up to find a tall young man with dark skin, dressed in a dark suit with a white shirt and a dark coloured tie standing beside Grandad. "Jamie." Grandad said "come here son" Jamie took the few paces necessary and stood immediately in front of his Grandad "I've got some important things to attend to" said Grandad "this young man will look after ye for a while, is that ok?"

Jamie nodded "Hello Jamie" said the young man. "My name is Lenny," and at that he held out his hand for Jamie to shake, of which Jamie obliged him.

"Now mind you don't get into any mischief," said Grandad before he walked off.

"I won't" said Jamie.

"Don't worry sir I'll look after him. "OK," said Lenny turning to Jamie, "what do you want to do? How about, if I show you around a bit to start off with?"

"Yes please." said Jamie.

"Ok follow me then," said Lenny and led Jamie off down the hall.

Lenny asked Jamie what he thought of the place. "It's amazing, but can you tell me how it works?"

"How what works?" Replied Lenny

"This building" said Jamie "how is it floating in the air?"

"Oh that" said Lenny stopping to think for a moment before smiling, bending down, and saying to Jamie in a whispered voice "It don't do, to ask too many questions around here, there's a lot of stuff I don't exactly understand myself, except to say … its magic."

"Magic?" replied Jamie

"Yeah you've heard of magic haven't you?" said Lenny

"Of course I have" said Jamie.

"Well then, that's what's holding the building up," laughed Lenny. He then stopped laughing and turned to Jamie "You do believe in magic don't you?"

"Well" … said Jamie "I'm not too sure."

"WHAT!" said Lenny "If you don't then this whole place might go crashing down to the ground if. Magic is what keeps the world turning." Lenny then stopped walking, his eyes widened and his mouth opened slightly "Wait, feel that?" he said

"Feel what?" said Jamie

"That slight shudder in the floor," replied Lenny.

"I can't feel anything," said Jamie.

"Are you sure?" said Lenny.

"Yes." Jamie said.

"Well… I hope your right. Because when this floor shakes it means that we have a non believer in our midst and the only way to save the building from crashing down to earth is to dump them overboard."

Jamie looked up at Lenny and said "you're kidding…right."

"No" replied Lenny. "Why do you think we got the hole in the floor?"

"What hole?" Jamie asked.

"The hole in reception" Lenny said.

"You mean the hard light chamber?" Jamie asked.

Lenny looked at Jamie "wow smart kid. Knows all about hard light and stuff ok then let's go and see."

"Go where" asked Jamie.

"To the hole in the floor" said Lenny.

"Why" asked Jamie.

"To do the walk of faith, we do it to all unbelievers," replied Lenny

"Explain" said Jamie.

"Well... what we do is we make them walk across it. If you're a believer the building likes you and you can cross it just like a regular concrete floor. But if you're a non believer PHEEEE!!! Its 2000 floors down before the sudden stop at the bottom and you're just a stain on the pavement. Would you like to take the test?" Lenny bent over and grinned right in Jamie's face as he said this.

Jamie grinned right back at Lenny and said. "I've already passed that test thank you very much."

Lenny stood back and then said "really...when."

"Earlier." Jamie replied.

"Ok! Well no harm in just making sure" said Lenny. "Come on we'll do the test again just to make sure," then Lenny took hold of Jamie's hand and pulled him around leading him back to the 'hole in the floor.'

Jamie yanked his hand out of Lenny's and said loudly. "NO WAY" and then backed away, looking quite scared.

Lenny looked at Jamie and then said "you know... you need to learn how to lighten up," and as he said that he burst out laughing loudly, almost doubling over and falling on the floor. Jamie realised that he had been fooled. His face blushed bright red as slowly a huge grin spread out all over his face and he too burst out laughing.

"Seriously though, that is a cool experiment" said Lenny.

"Experiment?" asked Jamie.

"Yes, an experiment" replied Lenny.

"What exactly do you mean by experiment?" asked Jamie.

"Like I said, it's an experiment, a trial, a test model," answered Lenny.

"So you mean that I've been jumping up and down on a test model? Something that has not been fully examined and made completely safe?" asked Jamie.

"Yeah, that's about it," answered Lenny.

"It could be dangerous," said Jamie. "What if it failed when someone was walking on it?"

"It very often fails," Lenny replied. "That's why you never find anyone walking on it."

Jamie felt the blood drain from his face. "Bloody Hell!" he thought.

Jamie followed Lenny down another corridor and through a door and into a large office, where lots of different people were working at desk. They looked very busy with phones ringing and people talking. In one corner, there was a group of people all huddled around a huge map of the world which hung on the wall, one of the people was pointing to the map at various places and commenting to the others (about what Jamie could not hear, but it all looked very serious.) They continued to walk through the office until they reached the far side where there was another door which they walked through and into a smaller office where a smartly dressed woman sat working at a computer terminal. She stopped working as Lenny and Jamie entered.

"Hi Lenny" said the woman, smiling.

"Hello Anne" replied Lenny "can I introduce you to Jamie?" he continued.

"Why hello there young man" said Anne to Jamie.

"Hello" replied Jamie.

"And what brings you here?" said Anne.

"I'm not sure," said Jamie in reply "except to say that I came here with my Grandad ...in a rocket."

"Well you must be someone very special and I'm pleased to meet you." Jamie said "thank you" before he was led out of this office and into another corridor. Jamie then followed Lenny into a small gymnasium.

"This is our recreation area." Lenny said, "I know it's not full size but we can get a pretty good workout by using the various machines." Lenny then pointed to the weight and treadmill machines that were around the room. There was also a space in the middle of the room where a small basketball court was marked out.

They left the gym and Lenny led Jamie to the rocket hanger. There were three different types of rockets in the hanger and all had people in overalls working on them. One had panels open along its side where a man with a spanner in his hand was reaching into and undoing something, another had a man underneath it with a light who seemed to be checking things out and the third one had huge pipes connected to it, like it was being filled up with fuel. "This is the garage," said Lenny, "this is where repairs and maintenance are carried out on the rockets." Just then something scurried past Jamie and jumped up at Lenny "Hey! Scamp, how ya doing buddy!" said Lenny to the small scruffy dog that was now barking and wagging his tail furiously and trying to jump up to lick his face. "Say hello to Jamie" The small scruffy dog had a quick sniff around Jamie's feet before jumping up onto Jamie's chest and excitingly licking his face. "I think he likes you," laughed Lenny while he too tried to dislodge Scamp from Jamie's face. They eventually managed the task when Scamp finally calmed down a bit. "He's a great dog, is he yours?" asked Jamie

"No he aint mine," said Lenny "in fact Scamp here don't belong to anyone here, He was found by someone out on a mission, somewhere, all messed up and hungry with no one to care for him. So he was brought here, washed and fed and looked after and now he's fit and healthy. He would make someone a great pet, providing they looked after him" and at that he gave Jamie a knowing wink. "Where does he sleep?" asked Jamie.

"He has a basket with a blanket in it somewhere around here," said Lenny. The pair of them looked around the room until Lenny spotted a basket in the corner of the hanger "Ah there it is," he said. Lenny, Jamie and Scamp walked over to it. As they neared the basket Scamp ran ahead and hopped into his basket, picked up a red rubber ball which was concealed inside and presented it to Jamie. "Looks like he wants to play ball," said Lenny.

Jamie took the ball from Scamp and bounced it a few times. Scamp wagged his tail in anticipation and excitement and began barking at Jamie expecting him to throw the ball. Jamie then threw the ball (not too far, though) and Scamp scurried away after it, caught it, and brought it back to Jamie. Just then, a beeping noise was heard. Lenny opened up his coat and took out a 'pager' which was clipped on to his inside pocket, pressed a switch, looked at the message screen, then said to Jamie "would you mind if I left you two here for a while, I have to make a call."

"Yes, that's ok Lenny, Scamp and I will just be here," said Jamie. Lenny smiled and walked away back towards the office from where they came. Jamie was enjoying playing with Scamp he didn't have a pet back home and began to wish that he could take Scamp back with him, when it came time to go home.

Jamie and Scamp were having a great time. It was a long time since anyone had paid this much attention to Scamp, He was scurrying to and fro after the ball barking with delight at every bounce. Jamie gave the ball an extra special hard throw this time and Scamp bounded after it. The ball hit the wall at the far side of the hangar, bounced off, hit a toolbox that was on the floor and ricocheted off in another direction behind one of the rockets with Scamp in hot pursuit. Jamie waited for a few seconds for Scamp to reappear. He didn't. A minute passed still no sign of Scamp. Jamie decided to look for him, 'he can't have gone far' thought Jamie. Jamie walked to the far side of the hangar calling "Scamp. Here boy" but Scamp was nowhere to be found. Jamie got down on his hands and knees and began to look under things but still no sign of Scamp. "Where on earth could he have got to? Jamie said to himself. Just then Jamie thought that he heard a faint bark coming from the inside of one of the rockets. This one had the rear cargo door open. Jamie walked up the ramp leading to the door and peered inside. It was quite gloomy as there was only a small light on. "Scamp" called Jamie. "Are you in here?" There came a sharp bark back in reply and as Jamie's eyes adjusted to the gloom. He could see the little dog frantically trying to retrieve the ball that Jamie had thrown and which had somehow bounced into the rocket and had become lodged between two wooden crates. "There you are" said Jamie and stepped off the ramp and into the cargo hold. "What's the matter boy, can't you get the ball out?" He walked to where Scamp was furiously scratching between the two crates. "All right let's have a look then" said Jamie as he bent down to peer into the gap. Suddenly the light went out and there was a muffled thud as the door behind him was closed shut. "Hey!"

shouted Jamie and ran back to where he guessed the door was and banged on the inside. "Hey let me out" he shouted and again banged on the inside of the door but it was no use, the entire inside of the cargo bay was covered with a thick padded material including the door and no matter how much Jamie shouted and banged no one could hear him. Jamie was trapped.

Outside the rocket the pilot was talking to another man "Is that it Jack?" asked the pilot.

"Yessir all loaded up and ready to go, except for your passengers, oh and here they come now." As they looked up five people came walking along the hanger led by Grandad and Rufus T Cody. All five people looked very serious as they boarded the rocket. Grandad paused in the doorway and looked around before entering; he had a concerned look on his face.

"Something wrong Mac?" asked Rufus to Grandad

"No" replied Grandad "nothing serious, ah just wanted a word with Jamie afore I went."

"Well it's a bit late now." Rufus said

"Aye so it is" said Grandad and at that turned and boarded the rocket, quickly followed by the other passengers.

– CHAPTER FOUR –

STOWAWAYS

Jamie gave up yelling and banging and sat down when he heard the whine of the engine start and sat down on something soft. Scamp gave a little whimper and came and sat on his lap. "Well Scamp, I don't know where we are going," he said staring into the dark. He was feeling a bit scared of not knowing where they are going and what's going to happen to them once they got there.

The rocket took off from New York and was on route to the Black Mountains, a journey which proved uneventful. They approached the Black Mountains very quickly to the delight of the passengers, who had had more than enough of Grandads singing during the short but very swift journey.

"Black Mountains dead ahead" came the pilots voice over the intercom. "Thank heavens for that" whispered Rufus to Mrs Bhattacharya.

"I'd sooner face a whole family of Dragons rather than listen to Macs singing again." Mrs Bhattacharya replied

"Sshh! He might hear you," but she could not keep herself from laughing as she said it.

Grandad and Rufus were great friends but neither of them could resist the temptation to 'wind up' the other whenever the occasion presented itself.

The pilot slowed the rocket down and was losing altitude when Rufus, Grandad, Liu Chung and Mr Yamamoto joined him in the flight cabin. The rocket passed close to villages which nestled in the foothills of the mountains and when they saw them, they all let out a loud gasp in horror, for as they got nearer they could see that most of the villages were just smoking ruins with all the buildings (or what was left of them) just burned and blackened shells. The fields of the surrounding countryside were just like a blackened and smouldering blanket and a thick fog hung over the mountains.

"It looks like they were hit hard," exclaimed Rufus.

"Oh all those poor people." said Mr Yamamoto.

"I hope they got everybody out in time," said Lui Chung.

"Let's go down for a closer look laddie," said Grandad to the pilot. The pilot nodded in acknowledgement and took the rocket down further.

They were now flying very low above what used to be a picturesque mountain village with 'Chalet' type buildings and ski lodges. There were no signs of life to be seen amongst the charred and blackened ruins. "Perhaps they're hiding in cellars or something," said Mrs Bhattacharya.

"Yes, let's land and take a quick look round for survivors," said Grandad.

They picked out a place to land right in the middle of the village square (as was) and they all got out. The air was thick with smoke and the smell of burning was everywhere. "We can cover more ground if we split up," said Rufus." So the party split up and began walking among the ruins shouting out "hello" and "anyone there" but there were no replies from the ruins. After a while they returned to the rocket and began to talk of departing when they heard a faint cry of "Help! In here" followed by a low thudding noise. "Shh! said Mrs Bhattacharya "Listen". They all stopped to listen then the pilot said, "I think it's coming from inside the rocket." They gathered closer to the rocket from which came a "Thud! Thud! Thud! "It's coming from inside the rocket," said two or three of them at the same time.

The pilot cautiously opened the cargo door and there sat Jamie, blinking in the now bright cargo bay with Scamp on his lap wagging his tail. "Well I'll be ... a stowaway," exclaimed Rufus. Grandad just stood opened mouthed for a few seconds before saying in an angry tone.

"Jamie... what the 'eck' are ye doing in there?"

"We got locked in," replied Jamie, "I have been shouting and banging for ages and no one took any notice," he continued (by now feeling a little angry himself).

The pilot helped Jamie down and Mrs Bhattacharya gave him a big hug and saying, "There, there Jamie it's all right you're quite safe now" and giving Grandad a scowl at the same time.

"What are we going to do with him?" asked Rufus.

"He can't stay with us," said Liu Chung "it's too dangerous." They all looked at Grandad.

"Ah well he'll just have to go back with the pilot," said Grandad. They all looked at Jamie. He was still feeling a bit sad and sorry for himself when Grandad said to him "well come on son, let's get you back home" and with that he put his arm around Jamie's shoulders and led him into the rocket.

Once everyone was on board the pilot said to everyone "I guess we'll have to drop the rest of you off first before I return with Jamie." Grandad nodded and the pilot went into his cabin.

"Ah see you've met Scamp." Grandad said to Jamie.

"Yes, isn't he great," replied Jamie "and he's very clever, he can do all sorts of tricks, watch." Jamie asked Scamp to "shake a paw" and Scamp duly obliged.

"Very good" said Grandad "he's come on very well. I would not have given you two pence for him when I first brought him back."

Jamie looked at Grandad. "You brought him back ... from where?"

"Oh let's see now," said Grandad... "Yes that was it I was in the jungle helping the Kernicknucs, a terrible to do, strange people though the Kernicknucs, if you can call them people?"

Jamie wondered what he meant by that remark and who or what where the 'Kernicknucs' but decided not to ask. He decided to ask about the village, "Grandad, what's happened to the village that we have just left?"

Grandad turned his head and looked at Jamie. "That son is what happens when you have just been paid a visit by your local Dragon and that is just one of the reasons why we must stop the 'Beastie' afore he does any more harm and even a lot worse."

"But how are you going to stop him" said Jamie.

"Well," said Grandad "hopefully that little job will be left up to the people who know what they're doing. Mr Liu Chung is pretty confident that he can persuade the Dragon to return to China with him. But our main task is to try and retrieve the 'stone' using wit and guile, and not do battle with Dragons. My name's James not George and I'm certainly no saint." Grandad then winked at Jamie and gave him a big smile.

The rest of the passengers were huddled around a map and were discussing passages and doorways, routes, and pathways up into and out of the dragons keep. There appeared to be some disagreements though. "OK, so how do we get in?" said Rufus.

"Well," replied Liu Chung the main entrance was sealed many ages ago, but there will be other secret entrances. The ones that we found are marked here, here and here," he said pointing to places on the map. "These too were sealed but dragons are very clever and can disguise the very biggest of openings." Rufus looked up from the map and looking slightly perplexed said "So we're looking for an invisible entrance, which no one knows about, which may be here or may not and which could be anywhere on the mountain? Well take a look out the window pal, that's a big mountain out there (even by Texas standards) we could be searching for months and never find it." This last remark caused some irritation among the rest of the party and arguments broke out among them. Mrs Bhattacharya silenced them by raising her voice (just slightly)

"Gentlemen Gentlemen please ... let Liu Chung continue." (The arguments stopped nearly at once)

"Thank you" said Liu Chung. "There has been a lot of mining activity on the mountain over the years (which ceased some years ago). However, whilst the mining was active, a tunnel was being cut here (Liu Chung now pointed to a place on the map) the miners who were digging broke through the rock and into a chamber which was part of the Dragons keep. This breakthrough was sealed and the mine abandoned many years ago. My proposal is to enter the Dragons lair through this tunnel and reopen the door that was made."

"Well that makes a lot more sense, I'll buy that! I apologise sir for going off the handle at you," said Rufus to Liu Chung. Liu Chung bowed slightly in acknowledgement. That settled Liu Chung took the map into the pilots cabin to give him directions of where to land.

It did not take long to reach the entrance to the mine and the rocket touched down safely on the small plateau immediately outside the entrance which had a huge rusty steel door which completely blocked the entrance. There was a small track which winded down from the mine which once must have been the main route up to the mine and there were rusty old bits of machinery discarded here and there amid the spoil heaps. They all got out of the rocket and began to unload their packs and things from the cargo hold. When this was done they walked towards the big steel door.

The door was about three metres high and was built to fit exactly into the entrance archway with not an inch of a gap anywhere to be seen. It had a huge padlock hanging on one side which was obviously locked. "Anyone got the key?" said Rufus and turned to face the others with a huge grin on his face. The others looked at each other shrugging their shoulders. Grandad walked up to the padlock, lifted it with his left hand, and then let it swing against the door. There was a loud metallic 'booming' noise as the padlock hit the door and the tunnel behind accentuated the noise and which sounded very like an ominous warning to Jamie.

Grandad took a couple of paces back, lifted up his walking stick, and pointed it at the lock. There was a sharp retort which sounded to Jamie like a sharp and high pitched 'CRACK and a blue flash shot out of the end of the stick, hit the padlock which immediately burst apart and fell with a heavy thud as it hit the ground. Rufus came over to Grandad; bent over the padlock looked at it for a second and then turned to Grandad and said, "You've killed it" before bursting out laughing.

Grandad just grinned and said, "Right help me get this door open."

Jamie was amazed. He was beginning to wish that he wasn't going home and that he could stay with his Grandad and 'see through' this adventure and be amazed some more. Grandad, Rufus, Mr Yamamoto, and Liu Chung all pulled at the massive steel door. Slowly, reluctantly the door started to open.

They pulled at the door until the gap got large enough so they could all pass through safely. All the team now stood inside the big wide tunnel and shone torches all around. It was damp and dark with water dripping here and there from the massive tunnel roof into pools that had formed over the years and stalagmites had began to form. There were also the remnants of rails with wooden sleepers which ran off deep into the gloom. It was a very foreboding place and Jamie couldn't help thinking that if there was such a thing as 'ghosts' then this is where they would live. The high spirits which he had had a few seconds ago about going off with his Grandad on adventures had now completely gone. Adventures were not always fun.

Jamie, Grandad and a few of the others went back outside. Grandad turned to Jamie "Well son, I didn't have time to say goodbye to ye proper back there but it's time to do so now". A loud clap of thunder which sounded very close interrupted him. Grandad and Jamie looked up at the towering mass of mountain above them but could only see a part of the way because of the mist that was swirling around the higher reaches. "That sounded very close." he said. There was another loud bang even louder and this time they felt the whole mountain shake slightly. The remainder of the team that were in the tunnel came racing out.

"What was that?" exclaimed Rufus. Everyone looked up at the mountain.

"I don't like the sound of this," said Liu Chung. Mrs Bhattacharya stood with her eyes closed and with her arms slightly outstretched then she opened her eyes wide and said. "There's something coming, quickly we must hide." There was another loud bang and the ground shook, this was followed by a loud rumbling noise. Small rocks and earth which had been dislodged by the banging began to fall down the mountain followed by bigger ones and then bigger still, until the whole plateau was being hit by a huge landslide. Massive boulders were now cascading down and whistling over their heads. "Everyone into the tunnel, quickly" shouted Rufus. Everyone ran towards the door of the tunnel grabbing pieces of equipment, backpacks and as many other items as they could and threw themselves inside. There they cowered in the blackness hands over heads protecting themselves from the hail of small rocks and earth that was raining down over them.

At last the shaking and banging stopped and so too did the shower of small rocks and dirt that was hitting them and the dust finally settled. Grandad called out "Jamie, are ye alright son?"

"Yes, I think so," said Jamie,

"Good lad," replied Grandad and stood up and held up his walking stick and holding it by the lower end thrust it in the air. The bulbous end glowed brilliantly with a bright yellow light which nearly lit up the whole tunnel. "Is everyone alright?" he called out. There were answers of "yes" and "think so" (as well as a bark from Scamp) as everyone got to their feet coughing and dusting themselves off.

"Are we all here?" Grandad called out again, they all looked at each other.

"The pilot is missing," said Mrs Bhattacharya.

"I saw him running towards the rocket" said Mr Yamamoto. There was a moment's pause before Rufus said, "Well let's hope he made it."

After collecting their thoughts together, they looked at the entrance door which had been slammed shut behind them and from which not the smallest bits of day light could be seen around its sides. Rufus tried pushing on it, which had not the slightest effect.

"Give us a hand will ya" said the big Texan. Everyone went to lend a hand and pushed as hard as they could against the huge door. Again, the door did not budge a fraction and they stopped. "Looks like we'll have to find ourselves another way out" said Rufus.

"Aye" said Grandad "and it looks like you've got your wish laddie," he said to Jamie.

"What do you mean?" Jamie asked.

"Well you did want to go on 'interesting adventures' didn't you?" replied Grandad.

"Well ... how did you know ... I mean ... yes, but crawling about in creepy tunnels wasn't one of them," said Jamie.

"Ah well if you are going to go on adventures, sometimes the path is chosen for ye," grinned Grandad.

They gathered their possessions together and led by Liu Chung they set off to find the tunnel which would lead them to the Dragons Lair. On route they tried to explain what it was that caused the landslide which blocked the entrance. "Thunder and lightning?" said Grandad.

"Rubbish," exclaimed Rufus "I aint seen no lightning strike which could bring down so much rock even in Texas."

"Earthquake then?" said Mr Yamamoto.

"No, I don't think so," said Mrs Bhattacharya. "I felt a very powerful presence. The rock fall was deliberately aimed and executed," she said. "Could it have been the Dragon?" she asked Liu Chung.

"Very probably," he answered. The group fell silent for a while as they heard his answer and pondered about their very formidable task ahead as they made their way along the tunnel.

They stopped every now and then when they reached other passageways to check with the map before continuing their journey deeper and deeper into the mine. They found the going was getting very hard and had to stop more frequently to rest.

"The air is getting very stale" said Rufus, "How much further?"

Liu Chung stopped to look at the map, "Not far now" he said "it should be just around the next tunnel." They continued for a further thirty minutes until they reached the point where the tunnel should lead to the Dragons lair. It was just a blank wall of solid rock.

"Is that it?" said Mr Yamamoto "no door or anything?" Liu Chung looked at his map and then back at the wall of rock. He then walked over to the rock and pressed himself against it, his arms outstretched. He stood in this position for a few seconds then stepped back, took off his back pack and placed it on the floor, opened it, rummaged inside it until he found what he was looking for and came out with a special looking light. He flicked it on. The light gave out a blue light and Liu Chung shone it against the wall of rock in front of them. He began to methodically 'sweep' the light against the hard rock in front of them. He began high up and gradually worked his way down to the floor of the tunnel. He slowly worked his way all along the rock for several metres until something caught his eye on the surface of the rock. He took a small brush from the inside pocket of his jacket and carefully brushed the surface of the rock. He then stood back and flashed the light over the surface that he had just brushed.

"It's here," he finally said.

The rest of the party now crowded around and looked at the place where Liu Chung was shining the blue light. There was a round crest which was illuminated by the light that Liu Chung held. The crest was round and approximately sixty centimetres in diameter. At its centre there was a spoked wheel and at the hub there was a Pyramid and in the centre of the pyramid was an eye. At each spoke there were symbols which Jamie learned later were representations of the four elements of Earth, Wind, Fire and water as well as figures of animals, fish, birds and mankind and around the edge of the wheel were the Latin words "*Circumvector Cognito Invenio Sapienta*" Which roughly translated into English as "Through Knowledge Discover Wisdom" although Jamie did not know this yet and it was also the motto of the High Council.

"Aye that looks like it," said Grandad. "Now all we have to do is find a way to get passed it and we're in." Rufus suggested that it should be 'blasted' open using dynamite.

"No we 'cannae' do that 'mon', the dragon would hear it, it would be like going up to his front door, banging on it and asking can we come in and steal his jewels. We have to break in without him knowing, steal the 'stone' back and away out again," said Grandad.

"That's a point," said Mr Yamamoto "we still have to find a way out, if ever we get to 'getting out again'. This last prospect put a gloomy mood over the party and it was a few minutes before anyone spoke again and of course it was Grandad.

"Right" he said, "does anyone know how the tunnel was sealed?" As he spoke he went up to the wall of rock and proceeded to tap on the surface with his stick and listened for any hollow sounds. There was none.

The adults all started to discuss matters concerning sealing tunnels and methods of construction and concealment and ignored Jamie, so Jamie just sat down and drew circles in the dust in the ground.

After a while Jamie had noticed that Scamp had wondered off and got up to look for him. He called out for him "Scamp...Scamp... here boy." There came a small bark in response and Jamie peered through the gloom. "Where are you boy?" Another bark sent Jamie in the right direction. He shone his torch around until the beam lit up Scamp. He was sniffing around a small rough hole in the tunnel wall away from the place where the others where. "What have you found boy?" Jamie bent down and looked into the hole. It went on for a metre or so then opened up wider. He thought he could feel a slight draught on his face and the air that was coming from the hole was fresher. Jamie thought that he would go and tell Grandad and the others. He got up and walked a few paces but Scamp would not come and began to crawl inside the hole and then disappeared inside it. Jamie went back to the hole, bent down, and shone his torch inside and once more in a hushed voice called "Scamp... you come back here... now." But of course Scamp did not come back. Jamie called for Scamp again in a muffled voice and waited and waited but he could not see him or hear him and was getting worried. Jamie went back to the others who were still talking amongst themselves. "Grandad, Grandad, come quickly," he said when he reached them.

"What is it son?" said Grandad (with some annoyance).

"Scamp has gone down a hole and hasn't come out again," exclaimed Jamie.

"OK, show me," said Grandad. Jamie led Grandad over to the hole and Grandad bent down low to have a look inside, putting his walking stick inside the hole, and lighting up the whole of the inside. "It goes along for quite a few metres" said Grandad "But I 'cannae' see any trace of yon daft dog."

The others came over to see what was going on. "What's happening?" asked Rufus.

"Well" said Grandad. "Scamp has found a way in but I'm not sure if we can all use it."

"But what about Scamp?" said Jamie "We've got to find him."

"OK son don't worry we'll get him back" said Grandad. They decided to send someone down the hole to retrieve Scamp but the only person that would fit (without getting stuck) was Jamie. Jamie volunteered straight away, so they tied a rope around Jamie's waist, gave him a torch and Jamie went into the hole head first.

The passage in the hole was quite a tight fit (even for Jamie) and it was difficult to crawl along at first. Eventually the passage got bigger and Jamie could move more quickly and he called out for Scamp as he moved further along.

The passage started to slope downwards quite steeply and Jamie had to be careful as not to go sliding down out of control. He thought he could hear Scamp barking and stopped to call out his name, "Scamp" ... Back came, the unmistakable sound of Scamp's bark. Jamie carried on slipping and sliding down the passage until he come to a small opening which had a drop of about six feet and there was Scamp wagging his tail and panting with excitement at seeing Jamie again. Jamie carefully managed to turn around in the tight opening and holding on to the bottom ledge of the passage gradually lowered himself to where Scamp was. Scamp was very pleased to see Jamie and he jumped up and licked Jamie's face. "There, there" said Jamie "are you all right boy? Good boy Scamp." Jamie then looked back at the passage from where he came and wondered how he was going to climb up to get back to the others carrying Scamp. He decided to look around for something that he could use as a stepladder, some large loose rocks or anything that he could pile up at the foot of the cave wall and use as a 'Step up.'

As Jamie searched he found that at the far end of the cave there was a large crack in the wall which gradually got larger and larger as it got nearer the bottom of the cave floor, so big in fact that Jamie could just about squeeze through (if he walked sideways). So not being able to find anything suitable to use as a stepladder Jamie decided to have a little explore. With Scamp tucked under one arm and with his torch in his other hand Jamie entered the crack.

It was hard going as the floor was not level and was open in several places so Jamie had to 'wedge' his feet in the crack in order to prevent himself from getting stuck by falling further down into the crack. Jamie was just about to give in and go back when his torch light reflected off something in the distance which glinted.
Thus curiosity got the better of him and he pushed on further into the crack. Jamie did not know it but that extra bit of curiosity which made him go those extra few feet would change Jamie's life forever. Call it madness, Dragon lust or just plain nosiness, it is what makes the difference between being thought of as being mad, and eccentric and going off all over the place and having all manner of weird and wonderful adventures and that of being regarded as being a 'rock solid sensible' person who wouldn't dream of doing anything that could be regarded as out of the ordinary.

As Jamie struggled through the crack he could see that he was coming out and entering a huge cavern. He stopped as he was on the very edge. He shone his torch down into the blackness. He thought that he could make out a smooth floor which stretched out for about thirty metres to the other side of the vast hall. He also realised that he was about ten metres up in the air from this floor peering through a crack in what was a side wall of the hall. The walls of the hall were very smooth and polished and this is what caused the light of the torch to reflect back at him. He shone his torch upward into a vast domed ceiling and then all around. There were pillars rising out of the floor here and there at regular intervals which ran on both left and right but how far they went he couldn't tell from his precarious position. He tried to adjust his feet to get a better view and also it was very tiring trying to hold onto Scamp who was beginning to get fed up of being held so tightly so he tried to jump down. He struggled to be released and Jamie was trying to keep a hold of him. "Steady Scamp you'll have us over" said Jamie. Hardly had the words left Jamie's mouth when he lost his footing and fell head first out of the crack and plunged down into the gloom.

How far Jamie fell he did not know, but what he did know was that he did not hit the bottom. The rope that his Grandad insisted he wore when he entered the hole now held him fast by the waist and he was swinging upside down in the dark. He had dropped the torch of course which now lay somewhere below him, broken no doubt. Jamie had managed somehow to hold on to Scamp who was busy licking Jamie's face and acting for the entire world like "wasn't that fun, and can we do it again."

Jamie was also aware of the searing pain in his sides and midriff where the rope had tightened to halt his fall. He couldn't hold on to Scamp for much longer so he manoeuvred Scamp so that his legs were facing the floor and said "I'm sorry Scamp I can't hold you much longer, I'm going to have to let you go."

Jamie let Scamp go and he dropped all of the way down to the floor (which was less than a metre away) Scamp looked at Jamie for a while before jumping up at him and licking his face. Jamie laughed, "OK boy, get down." Jamie struggled to get himself the right way up again but manage it he did. He just hung there for a short while. His eyes now adjusted to the gloom and he could see for a short distance. He could make out rubble on the floor and doorways leading off the main hallway. Jamie decided that he should free himself of the rope and tried to undo the knot but he couldn't. Jamie's weight was keeping the knot in the rope too tight and try as he might he just could not open it. So he just hung there for a while until suddenly Scamp jumped up and took hold of the end of the rope in his mouth and yanked it hard. The knot sprung apart and Jamie fell to the ground with a dull thud on his backside. Jamie took a few deep breaths and rubbed his aching sides. He then felt a cold wet nose in his face as Scamp came to him. "Thanks pal" said Jamie. "But, next time give me a bit of warning before you pull the rip cord. Ok."

The floor was very smooth and must have been very highly polished because when the dust was removed it still shone and although there was rubble strewn around here and there this place must have been very impressive in it's time. Jamie decided to wander around and walked out further into the hallway. He strained his eyes until they hurt as he peered into the gloom. He was completely disorientated. He had no idea which direction was which (apart from up and down and even about that he was in some doubt) So Jamie just sat down in the blackness and closed his eyes. Scamp joined him. The two of them comforted each other until they could be rescued.

As the minutes went by Jamie's eye sight seemed to become more accustomed to the darkness. As he looked around him there seemed to be a faint light coming from one direction and Jamie wondered whether it was just his imagination playing tricks on him such was the blackness. Jamie was now torn between going to see what the light was or to sit tight and wait until Grandad came and rescued him or, try to think of a way to get back to the others. He walked back to where he thought the rope hung only to find that the rope was no longer there. He searched by trying to 'feel' his way to it. After several minutes of this blundering about waving his arms around "Hey" Jamie shouted in a muffled sort of yell and repeated it a few times but it was too late. The others had obviously pulled the rope back through to them. "Now how are we going to get back to them?" Jamie said to Scamp as he peered upwards trying to locate the crack that they had fallen from.

Jamie strained his ears to listen if he could hear anything, he couldn't. He waited and just stood there looking upwards. He waited with his arms folded looking up, nothing again, and finally he waited with his hands in his pockets looking up. It didn't make any difference there was still nothing. (Scamp, meanwhile had decided that this game was boring and sat down, and after being bored of sitting he then lay down.) Finally Jamie looked at Scamp and said "Come on Scamp, I think we had better try and find our own way out, Lets go this way and see what that light is."

Jamie and Scamp set off towards the light. The floor sloped upwards slightly until it reached a flight of stairs going up. They climbed the stairs. At the top the hallway was narrower and Jamie could make out doorways and windows. This reminds me of a shopping mall, thought Jamie and walked over to investigate a doorway. Jamie didn't realise it but he was a very changed boy from the one which was frightened of ghosts when they first opened the entrance to the tunnel up on the side of the mountain. His spirit of adventure had won through and he was now walking along a dark and gloomy ancient passage investigating dark and scary places as though he was born to it. Scamp too was busy exploring, sniffing out things in things around things and then cocked his hind leg and 'peed' on them. "Scamp, you stop that, do you hear me," said Jamie in a scowling voice. Scamp just glanced at Jamie and then carried on with complete nonchalance.

Jamie and Scamp carried on the journey towards the light which was getting brighter all the time until they entered a huge round room with a massive dome in the middle. How high it was Jamie could only guess, it reminded him of the inside of St Paul's Cathedral in London (which he had visited with his parents). However, this was not the source of the light. That was coming from one of the smaller, but none the less, huge antechambers which joined the main dome. Jamie and Scamp walked toward the light and into a smaller room. It was round like the main one and the walls where made of a light coloured marble which shone beautifully as it bathed in the strange yellow light. In the middle of the room was a large round plinth and on it was a tall round column, which rose some five metres into the air. At the very top Jamie could make out a statue of a man in long robes and a long beard. He had one hand down by his side while the other was held out in front of him and in this hand he was holding something. This...something was the source of the light while coiled right around the column leading up was a huge scaly stone serpent creature. Its scales, matching the coloured marble of the column exactly. Seated all around the room against the wall there were stone statues of small squat grim faced men with beards and wearing helmets and chain mail armour. Each of their hands were placed one on top of the other atop of a broad sword which was placed upright between their knees. Jamie looked up at the light. He could see it clearly now as he moved to one side. It came from a large egg shaped stone which appeared to be floating in mid-air. The statues hand wasn't holding it at all.

Jamie stood and stared at the stone. It was beautiful and the light that came from it didn't glare or make you shield your eyes, in fact the opposite was true. The light was quite hypnotic and the more Jamie looked at the stone the deeper he wanted to look. Jamie could hear Scamp barking but could not bring himself to see what he was barking at. He thought he heard Scamp give out a 'yelp' but again Jamie took no notice. All Jamie could think about was the beautiful light. He began to climb up the column using the scaly beast as a ladder.

Jamie gradually made his way up and up nearly slipping a few times as the scales was very smooth. Sweat began to appear on Jamie's brow as he neared the top of the column and his heart thumped as his hands gripped the top of the base of the statue. Jamie placed his foot on top of the base and slowly raised himself up so that he was now stood against the legs of the statue, which was taller then it looked from the ground. Jamie's head was about level with the statue's waist and he inched his way around to the front to where the statue's right arm was held outstretched with its hand open, palm upwards. And there hovering motionless about forty centimetres above this empty palm was the prize. It was his. All he had to do was reach up to the outstretched arm. Grip it. Swing up and...it was then that Jamie woke up from the trance which held him as he felt his foot slip from the plinth of the statue and he plunged down, head first towards the ground. Jamie was just about to let out a scream when his fall was halted just an arms length from the cold hard stone of the ground.

He was caught, held tight. He could feel its cold steely grip tighten around his neck and body. Then the grip slackened and Jamie could turn his head slightly to one side and as he did so he stared straight into a huge fiery eye.

- CHAPTER FIVE -

THE WAY IN

Grandad and the others watched as Jamie disappeared down the hole in the wall. Rufus had attached one end of a rope around Jamie's middle and the other end had been tied around Grandad's waist. They just watched as the rope slithered metre by metre down the hole after Jamie.

"I do hope he'll be alright," said Mrs Bhattacharya.

"Of course he'll be alright" answered Grandad, "He's a McGregor."

Jamie had been gone for some minutes and some of the group began to express concern that Jamie had not returned. But the rope continued to slowly 'snake' it's way down the hole so they assumed that Jamie was alright and the conversation changed to talking about what they were going to do next and how they were going to get passed the sealed entrance and into the Dragons lair. Suddenly the last few metres of rope began to shoot through the hole until it was halted by Grandad. However, being tied to Grandad's waist, the rope 'yanked' Grandad toward the hole and he ended up being flattened against the rock face.

The others frantically tried to pull Grandad away from the rock as he was in no position to do it himself. "Are you all right Mac?" asked Rufus.

"Pah plink plo" came back the muffled reply from Grandad whose face was being tightly pressed against the cave wall above the hole.

They remained like this for a couple of minutes, all pulling and straining until suddenly they were all propelled backwards as the weight on the other end gave up and they all ended up in a heap on the floor all on top of each other. Mr Yamamoto was the first to recover and he grabbed the rope and frantically began to reel it in until the end of it shot out of the hole and hit Grandad smack dab right in the face (who was just picking himself up again before the rope knocked him down again) Mrs Bhattacharya raced to the hole shone her torch down it and yelled "Jamieeeeee" and then listened. There was no sign of Jamie and she could not hear any reply. There were many shouts and yells by the group down the hole to try and resume contact but in the end they assumed that Jamie had fallen down somewhere and was lying hurt and unable to shout back.

Rufus then picked up the end of the rope and looked closely at it. "Hey Mac, take a look at this" he said to Grandad and handed Grandad the end of the rope. Grandad took the rope and examined it carefully ... "Well, what do you think?" asked Rufus.

"It's not been cut," said Grandad

"Yes you're right," said Rufus. "And it's not been snapped."

"Well it's no use us sitting around here guessing, we've got to get passed yon entrance and find out" said Grandad.

The group now all walked over to where the sealed doorway was and several of them tried to get the door open by reciting lots of 'opening' spells and incantations in a variety of differing languages. They tried pushing on it, pulling it, kicking it. Grandad tried hitting it with the end of his stick but the 'bolts' of blue lightning that this produced just bounced off and ricocheted around the passage just missing people's heads (much to their consternation)

"Hey! cut it out Mac" Rufus cried out as a blue lightning bolt flew passed his head, missing him by inches. Grandad just grinned and said "Oh! Sorry Rufus" and stopped. Liu Chung approached the wall and was reciting all manner of things in Chinese and other languages and dialects now long forgotten and after half an hour or so he gave up and sat down upon a rock, his head bowed. Grandad, who was now sitting on the floor a few metres back from the door shook his head and said "Hang on a moment. There must be a clue in the seal."

"What do you mean?" asked Liu Chung.

"Well...I remember reading something in the library. It was years ago I was talking with a member of the sealing team and he was telling me how they put clues in the seal to show you how to reopen it. We need to find the seal again and examine it more closely," said Grandad. They all began to search franticly at the wall and after a few minutes there came a loud "Ha Ha" from Rufus. The group scurried over and Liu Chung shone his blue light over the area. Sure enough the seal came into view and they all stood back to look at the detail, which now stood out from the rock. They all stared hard at the seal and no one spoke for several minutes until at last Rufus spoke up. "Okay... anyone any ideas?"

Grandad replied, "Nothing jumps out that's for sure."

"The clues will be very discreet and subtle," said Mrs Bhattacharya. "There will be very small changes to something which on first impressions seem, very normal." Everyone stared hard again at the seal and silence befell them.

After roughly half an hour Grandad spoke. "This is getting us nowhere. We are wasting time. Jamie could be lying seriously hurt and needing medical attention. We must hurry this up."

"You are right," said Mr Yamamoto. "There must be another way of getting passed the entrance without"....

"Wait" said Liu Chung. "There is something different in the seal. Look at the figure of the Man." Everyone now looked intently at the small figure at the bottom of the wheel. "I don't see anything different," said Rufus.

"Look at his arms" said Liu Chung.

"What about them?" Asked Rufus.

"They are outstretched, pointing," said Liu Chung.

"So, don't they always" said Rufus.

"No, they don't. Normally they just hang down by his sides. Think about the big seal which hangs at Cloud base." said Liu Chung.

"He is correct," said Mrs Bhattacharya. "He is pointing at the fish with his left arm and the bird with his right"

"Ok" said Grandad "Now what does it mean?"

There then followed some debate about the possible meaning of the figures of the fish, bird and the man. Until, Liu Chung said "There must be some more figures. Look around for more." Everyone began to search for more signs. It did not take long before there was a cry from Rufus.

"Look here, I found a figure. But it's not a fish or a bird." They all came over to look at what Rufus had found. It was a figure of an insect. An ant to be exact, carved in the rock.

"We must find the bird and the fish," said Liu Chung. "They are of the utmost importance."

A few seconds later Grandad shouted, "Bingo, it's the fish, over here on the ground." They scraped the dust and dirt away to reveal the full figure of the fish carved into the rock which was about thirty centimetres long and inside of a circle. The gloom, which had hung over the group suddenly lifted at this discovery and the search for the bird continued with renewed vigour.

They found the other symbols that were on the wheel and then suddenly they found the bird, which again was located on the ground about four metres away from the fish.

"Now what happens?" said Grandad obviously very eager now to get the entrance open. Everyone now looked at Liu Chung in expectation. Who in turn looked back at them? "What?" said Liu Chung.

"Well what do we do now?" said Grandad.

"I don't know," said Liu Chung.

"It may be a pressure release system?" said Mr Yamamoto. "Press down on the bird" Grandad stepped upon the bird...Nothing happened. "Try the fish then," said Mr Yamamoto again nothing.

"Wait a minute" said Rufus "try them both together." Both Grandad and Mrs Bhattacharya pressed the bird and the fish with their feet...Nothing.

Rufus then went over to Mrs Bhattacharya and asked her to "please stand aside Ma'am" Rufus then stood with his considerable weight upon the fish. It sank down about fifteen centimetres but still no entrance appeared "Quick a couple of 'ya', jump on the bird," cried Rufus. Grandad and Mr Yamamoto jumped together on the carved figure. It sank down just like the fish. There then came a low rumbling noise as some underground mechanism turned. Then there came a couple of quite loud metallic clicks before the floor in front of the rock face suddenly swung downwards sending those standing there tumbling down into the dark hole which had appeared. Rufus, Grandad, and Mr Yamamoto who were taken by surprise also lost their balance and went blundering into the hole after them. They all went slithering and sliding, down the stone ramp in the pitch blackness until they hit level ground with a thud.

Grandad was first to get to his feet and lit up his stick "Come on" said Grandad picking up his belongings, throwing them on his back and setting off down the new passage "we have no time to waste, we've a boy to find" The rest of the group quickly picked up their packs and followed Grandad into the new passage.

The passage was smaller than the others they had come down and seemed to get narrower the deeper they got until eventually they had to follow each other in single file. They suddenly came to the end of the passage and Grandad stopped. He put out his light on his walking stick; told the others to extinguish theirs and whispered to the others to "be verrrry quiet" As quietly as he could Grandad walked to the end of the passage and slowly poked his head through the narrow opening. It took a few moments for his eyes to grow accustomed to the gloom and after a few moments of peering up and down and round about he took his stick and held it aloft out in the open. The bulbous end lit up the whole area around him and he gave a small gasp as he saw the great hallway that was all around him. However, like Jamie, he found himself roughly ten metres up in the side of the wall looking down. "Wassamatta" whispered Rufus who was right behind him. "There's no floor," said Grandad "we'll need a rope to get down"

"Wait" said Liu Chung "I think it would be wiser for me to go down first and take a look around just to make sure that it is safe to continue." Grandad argued that they were wasting time and needed to get down quickly to find Jamie but the others disagreed and decided that Liu Chung should go first and check things out.

Liu Chung was lowered to the floor. He untied the rope and set about looking around. The others remained silent as they watched Liu Chung's torch flash here and there about the walls and floor. They saw it stop for a moment and they saw Liu Chung crouch down to examine something on the floor, then he came back to the rope and signalled for the others to follow him. Rufus went down next followed by Mrs Bhattacharya, then Mr Yamamoto who asked Grandad "how are you to get down when there is no-one to hold the rope?" Grandad just grinned at him and said

"Dinnae' fash' 'yersel' laddie, I'll manage." After safely lowering Mr Yamamoto down Grandad tied one end of the rope around his walking stick and wedged it into a crack in the wall of the passage, tugged on it a couple of times to ensure that it was secure and then proceeded to lower himself down to meet the others. At the bottom Rufus asked "What about your stick?" and pointed upwards with his thumb, at which Grandad gave a short tug on the rope and somehow his stick (still with rope attached) came sailing down out of the dark and hit Rufus square on the top of the head "OWWWW!! He yelled to which everyone turned on him and went "SSSSSSHHHHHHH!"

Grandad untied the rope coiled it up carefully up and slung it over his shoulder. He then rejoined the others who were gathered around something on the floor "What is it" said Grandad.

"Look" he said, "and look here also" Liu Chung shone his torch now on the floor and there all around was the unmistakable footprints of Jamie and also of Scamp's paw prints which they followed to the middle of the hallway and which then led off up the slope in the direction of the faint glowing light. "Well at least we know that he survived the fall," said Grandad

"Yes! And he has gone walkabout" said Mr Yamamoto.

The Group was fascinated by the place that they were in. "What do you make of it" said Rufus to Liu Chung "I didn't know dragons were capable of building such places, it must have been some place in its day."
"Dragons are capable of many wonderful things," said Liu Chung "unfortunately they are also capable of death and destruction too only this is not of dragon making. The Dragon came here after it was built to take it from people who lived here." Grandad said that it was a terrific feat of mining whoever had built it and the local legends say that the people who built this place were Gnomes, terrific miners, who built palace's inside of mountains before the time of men, but who were awfully greedy and would store vast wealth of gold and jewels which would unfortunately attract the likes of Robber Barons, thieves and of course Dragons and thus bring about their downfall.

They decided to follow Jamie's footprints but decided against calling out Jamie's name in case the Dragon might hear them. Grandad let out a small laugh, "Ha! Yon dragon is probably well aware that were here after all the wailing that Rufus did when ma wee stick hit him on the head"
Rufus turned on Grandad "Oh! Yeah! Well let me hit you on the head with it Mac and let's see if you don't cry out."
Rufus then tried to grab hold of Grandad's walking stick and a struggle ensued between the pair before the others broke it up. Mr Yamamoto was scathing in his criticism of the pair saying that "your behaviour is most unprofessional" after which Rufus and Grandad looked at each other and then stifled a laugh behind Mr Yamamoto's back.

They reached the place where a flight of stairs led up to the other level and which was the way that Jamie went but at the bottom Mrs Bhattacharya stopped and closed her eyes, took a sharp intake of breath and shivered a little. "What's the matter?" asked Grandad. It took a moment for Mrs Bhattacharya to reply, "Grimfell is near" she said.
"Yes, I feel him too," said Liu Chung.

- CHAPTER SIX -

GRIMFELL

Jamie just stared into the huge eye. He was completely caught. He could feel the power of the creature which held him. It was like being held in a huge steel vice. Jamie was completely at the mercy of the Dragon. This huge fiercesome head was no more than half a metre from Jamie's face. The Dragon then closed his eyes and took a huge sniff of Jamie, at which Jamie felt he was going to be sniffed right up Grimfell's huge nostrils. The dragon then uncoiled himself from the pillar and placed Jamie gently on the ground and backed away and proceeded to walk around the room sniffing the air and talking to himself saying ... "Man-child ... yes ... definitely ... and others." Jamie watched, as the great monster's body seemed to flow around the room until the Dragons head was again level with Jamie.

Nothing could have prepared Jamie for this moment. All the drawings and pictures of 'made up' dragons that he had seen in books were nothing like this magnificent creature that now stood just a few metres away. The Dragons head was about a metre and a half wide with a long snout and flared nostrils. There were also horns about his head that started as small 'bumps' in between his eyes on the forehead in a 'v' shape, all pointing backwards and gradually getting larger as the further towards the back of the head they got until they ended magnificently in huge long horns that swept backwards. His eyes were of a brilliant emerald green colour with a fiery red elongated pupil that ran vertically in the middle, above which long eyebrows ran out from the top and swept back also for about a metre. He had small scales which seemed to start from the tip of his snout and gradually grow in a backwards looking pattern, again getting bigger as the further back they got, the biggest ones being about his body. Jamie expected to see wings upon his back but there wasn't any, which surprised him. The colour of the dragon was hard to determine in the yellow light of the room but Jamie guessed that it started off as being a dark green colour at the top and gradually got lighter the further towards his underneath that you looked. But not only that, the colours seemed to change hue as he moved about.

"What is your name?" Grimfell suddenly said to Jamie (snapping him out of his trance like state). Jamie blinked a few times before mumbling "Jamie." The dragon thought about this for a moment and then asked, "How did you get in here?"
Jamie hesitated before replying, "I fell in"
"And your companions, did they fall in also?" asked Grimfell. Jamie thought quickly about the question and decided that it might not be wise to tell him that he had others with him. "What others?" said Jamie. At this reply the dragon roared loudly and rounded on Jamie bringing his head closer to Jamie's face and said in a low menacing voice "Don't lie to me man-child, I know very well that there are others for I can smell them and sense them along with your smelly pet dog." Jamie was suddenly reminded of Scamp and said "Scamp, where is he?" To which Grimfell replied
"Oh don't worry Jamie; (he said in mock concern) he fled when I came. He has probably gone back to warn your friends but I'll catch up with him later. It's a good job that I have had a good feast of goats, sheep, and cattle from the village or he would now be eaten. Now, tell me what you are doing here and where you come from and I don't want any of your lies for I know all about men and their cruel wicked ways."

Jamie swallowed hard and was very, very frightened but he kept his wits about him and then stammered.
"W...W...W...Well, m...m...my c...c...c...Companions and I were exploring the old mines in the side of the mountain when a massive landslide blocked us in, we were trying to

find a way out when I fell down a hole and ended up here. I'm very sorry to have troubled you G, G, G, and Grimfell and if you don't mind I think I should be getting along now, g g g goodbye." At that Jamie turned and began to walk towards the doorway to go out when a massive scaly three clawed foot slammed down in front of him.

"Oh! Don't be so hasty my little friend, you are my guest. I wouldn't dream of letting you go so soon," said Grimfell. "Now then, why don't you sit down here and tell me all about yourself and how it is that you came by my name, for I have not mentioned it yet." Jamie felt a right fool, how could he have been so careless, (Jamie thought to his self. Well my lad, you are going to have to do some mighty fast talking to get out of this) What Jamie did not realise was, that dragons are very clever at getting people to tell them exactly what it is that they want to know, even if you don't want to tell them, and it takes a very skilled dragon talker to resist their will for even a little of the time.

Jamie sat down on the plinth and placed his arms around his knees.

"Now man child, tell me what you know of me," said Grimfell.

"I don't know a lot" said Jamie "only that you have escaped from somewhere and have stolen a stone which is very precious." The dragon closed his eyes and stretched his head up. A low grumbling sound came from deep inside his throat and whiffs of smoke came from his nose along with a terrible smell. He then whirled his head around and roared "LIES!" ... the stone does not belong to man. It was hidden ... it wasn't meant to be found yet" The dragon seemed to calm down now, and his voice grew soft and tender.

"Come...tell me what you know of us," he said.

"Well there is not much to tell really" began Jamie. "You're very dangerous creatures who can fly and breathe fire and that nobody really believed you existed. You are a mythical creature...oh! And you also eat people"

There was a long period of silence before Grimfell spoke. "Is that it? Is that it?"He repeated His voice now rose very loud. "Three million years of history of Dragon lore and all we end up with is that we never existed. We were the stuff of some ones imagination. A creature to scare the children with in your fairy tales and a creature to be slain as sport by your so called heroes. That's it isn't it. Oh yes that's it isn't it. A mad dangerous monster has escaped it must be destroyed before it runs amok and kills everyone." The Dragon had now finished his rant and now came closer to Jamie. Is that what they told you Jamie? It is isn't it? Oh yes that's what this means. They mean to slay me. Well I'll show them. We'll see who dies." Grimfell's eyes seem to get narrower as he finished and the redness in his eyes burned brighter.

"All that you have heard about us is lies. My Dear Jamie, Dragons (as you call us) were here before man, when the earth was young. We it was who calmed the seas, and prepared the land for the coming of man. Planted the forests and rid the world of many very dangerous creatures that did not want to share the earth. We taught men very many things. Take these halls, in which we now sit, they were once very beautiful. The ceiling was once very blue and in the evenings it would shine with brilliant white diamonds like the stars in the heavens. We it was who showed these Gnomes and later men how to create such beauty. However they were very cruel and wicked. They delved deep into the earth and despoiled the land. They tunnelled with their machines and blasted the earth. They hacked down trees with their iron axes and would not share their gold and other treasures that they stole from us. They made weapons, and had huge armies and they made war upon us and many of our kind were killed. When man first came, we rejoiced at their coming for they would treat us kindly and with respect. But we were betrayed, because men would trick us, then they told lies about us, they would hunt us down and slay us to eat our brains because they believed to do so would make them strong, brave, and wise. Now there are none left save me. I myself was hunted down, driven from my home, captured, and placed in chains for decades. These now broken and empty halls was once the last refuge of a poor and desperate creature who only wanted to be left alone to live out the rest of his days in peace and free from harm. But man wanted me dead, but somehow they spared me and I was imprisoned, forever, never again to feel the wind in the sky or to bathe in the clear fresh oceans with my brothers."

Dragons talk like this because they have a completely twisted way of trying to justify their cruel and selfish behaviour. However, because they can cast spells upon people just by talking to them, Jamie was caught up in the dragons spell and he believed what the Dragon had said and felt very sorry for him.

Jamie stood up "you poor thing" said Jamie "I didn't know that you had suffered so much. I thought that dragons were nasty creatures that would terrify people and eat them."

Grimfell looked at Jamie with his eyes wide and said, "Well then, I told you that men told lies didn't I. I haven't hurt you have I?" Jamie agreed, then something stirred for a moment inside Jamie and he said "But why did you steal the stone?"

A menacing look came into the Dragons eyes for a few seconds before he replied.

"I took only what is mine. It is the past, present, and the future"

Jamie asked him what that meant and then Grimfell said, "As long as I hold the stone, I control my destiny, my future"

Jamie looked up at the stone "Is that the stone" he asked and pointed towards the light that hovered still high in the air.

"It is indeed," answered the dragon. "But what will happen if you don't have the stone" said Jamie.

Grimfell's eyes narrowed as he looked at Jamie and said, "The time of the Dragon will come to an end."

The dragon now sniffed the air and said "Ahh! more 'guests' have arrived" and went out into the main hallway before stopping and saying to himself "A little welcoming party I think" and then turned and went back to where Jamie was still sitting in the smaller room.

"Your companions will be arriving shortly and I've got a little surprise for them," said Grimfell. He then walked over to the end stone statue of the small squat grim looking men which were aligned around the room and said something in a language which Jamie did not understand (but it sounded as though he was making a spell) after which, the dragon did breath a white smoke on to the statue.

The smoke drifted from statue to statue and as it did so each of the statues eyes opened and glowed fiery red. When the last of the statue's eyes had opened Grimfell raised his voice and said.

> "Cold be ice and cold be stone,
> And cold be dead just skin and bone.
> Never more to feel the sun,
> In your halls of Kundra Dun,
> Awake from death with this breath
> Awake! Again from your sleep,
> Slay the foe that among you creep.
> That dared to enter your sacred keep"

At this, all the statues stood up from their seats and marched single file out of the room and out into the larger room. When the last of them had cleared the doorway they stopped, spun upon their heels in a left turn, and then marched abreast, (swords held at the ready) down the hallway.

CHAPTER SEVEN

ESCAPE AND EVADE

Grandad took hold of Mrs Bhattacharya's arm and helped her to the top of the stairs where they stopped for a moment "I'll be fine now, thank you" she said to Grandad "What did you feel" he asked her.

"It's very hard to describe," She answered "there were a lot of different emotions but anger and revenge I felt the most. His will is very powerful. He will make a formidable opponent."

They continued on their way up the great hallway, just checking every now and then for Jamie's footprints when Liu Chung stopped everyone and told them to listen. At first they could not hear anything and Grandad was just about to make a comment when a sound caught his ear. The noise was very low at first but seemed to be getting louder it was regular and sounded like marching feet, only well, different. "What do you think it is?" said Mrs Bhattacharya to no one in particular

"I don't know" replied Rufus "but I don't like it"

Grandad remarked, "It's coming this way though."

They continued to listen and stare towards the direction of the noise. Mr Yamamoto said to them "All stay here, while I scout ahead" Then, surprisingly very quickly and silently Mr Yamamoto ran on ahead and disappeared into the gloom. He flitted in and out of the darkness taking what cover there was behind the tall pillars. He then heard a running noise which slowed, as it got nearer. Yamamoto pinned himself behind one of the pillars, he could hear a sniffing noise which got steadily closer and closer until suddenly a small animal came out of the gloom and began to sniff around the pillar that Yamamoto was hid behind. Mr Yamamoto's heart was beating very fast and he wanted to jump out and run away, but he stayed. The small animal then came and sniffed right at Mr Yamamoto's feet. He looked down at the creature. It was Scamp who just looked up at Mr Yamamoto wagging his tail. Mr Yamamoto let out a huge sigh of relief and bent down to pick Scamp up. "Scamp, where have you been boy? Where is your little friend Jamie?" Scamp just gave a little bark in reply before being 'shushed' by Mr Yamamoto. Still carrying Scamp, Yamamoto ventured out further along the hallway and all the while the heavy sound of marching feet got louder. He ducked behind a large chunk of rock that had fallen down from somewhere and straining his eyes peered into the darkness until finally he could just make out the strange and frightening eyes that belonged to the marching line of short squat menacing figures that were coming towards them.

He was gone less than a minute before he returned. "Whaddiyasee" asked Rufus.

"I found this," said Mr Yamamoto holding out Scamp. Scamp was fussed over by all the party and then Grandad asked, "Any sign o Jamie?"

"No I'm afraid not," said Yamamoto "but I saw eyes."

"Just eyes?" asked Rufus

"No, not just eyes, but eyes mainly," said Mr Yamamoto.

"What sort of eyes" asked Liu Chung.

Grandad was beginning to get agitated "Will you tell us what ye saw man, instead o all this blather about eyes!" An argument would have started amongst them if not for the intervention (yet again) of Mrs Bhattacharya who calmed things down. "Right" she said, "please continue Mr Yamamoto" (and he did).

"I saw a line of men, short, but thick set men"

"With eyes" interjected Rufus

"Yes," replied Mr Yamamoto "big bright red shiny evil eyes."

Grandad asked him. "How many were there?"

Mr Yamamoto replied "eyes or men?"

Grandad raised his stick to strike Mr Yamamoto but was stopped by Rufus.

"Men of course ye daft beggar" said Grandad

"Ten or twelve" replied Yamamoto nervously grinning from ear to ear.

"What are we going to do?" said Mrs Bhattacharya.

"I don't know. Any ideas anyone?" answered Rufus.

"What are these men?" Asked Liu Chung "Are they a threat to us? Do they know that we are here? Can we hide from them until they have passed?" Nobody could answer Liu Chung's questions but Rufus said, "I'm not normally the kind o guy that runs away from a fight but it seems to me that we don't know who or what these here critters are, or what they want. So it might be sensible like to keep our heads down until such time as we know what we're up against"

They all agreed that this was the best thing to do, so they decided to try and hide from 'whatever' it was that was heading their way. They discovered a doorway not far from where they were in which a stairway went up and curved round but they decided that this was not the time to explore, however there was lots of debris laying around nearby and so they hid among this and waited for the arrival of the marching men.

They did not have long to wait before they could clearly see a line of red fiery eyes approaching, their marching feet getting louder and louder until they were within a few feet of Grandad who was hidden behind a large chunk of fallen ceiling and he held his breath until he thought he would burst. Finally, the line of stone men marched on past them and down the hallway, the echo of their feet getting further away.

It took a couple of minutes before any of the group dared to show their faces again and it was Grandad who finally bobbed his head up, took a few careful steps out from behind his hiding place and looked good and long in the direction on the receding footsteps.

"Ye can aw come out now, I think they've gone" The others all appeared from out of their hiding places breathing sighs of relief "Now what in the Sam Hill was that" exclaimed Rufus. The others all expressed that they had never before seen such a thing except Liu Chung who told them that it reminded him of something that he had seen in China, and told them all about some ancient Emperors who had built huge terra cotta armies and had them buried with them when they died.

"I think we should move on," said Grandad." The others agreed and moved around to gather up their belongings. Rufus was the first to gather his gear and moved to the middle of the hallway. While he waited for the others he bent down to stroke Scamp who was looking along the hallway in the direction of where the marchers went. Rufus stroked his head and said "Hello there fella. Howya getting along?" Scamp just bared his teeth and growled. Rufus was a little taken aback by Scamps behaviour and said "Whoa! there boy, I'm only trying to be friendly" But Scamps growl was not aimed at Rufus for there coming back towards them and now only a few metres away was the menacing figure of a stone warrior, his eyes a blazing red and with his sword held aloft ready to charge and strike.

"Oh! Oh! ... Hey guys! ... Ol red eyes are back" shouted Rufus to the others. The others whirled round to find themselves being singled out for a sudden and sneaky charge by the stone warriors. Rufus just managed to dodge the downward 'chop' from his assailant's sword as it lunged towards him and he jumped behind a large boulder closely pursued by his attacker. The others were all busy dodging and scurrying around weaving away from the deadly blows of the warriors. There were shouts and yelps from the members of the team as they ducked and dived and attempted to defend themselves. Rufus aimed a mighty punch at his attacker and it landed right on target, square on the jaw. The stone warrior never even flinched as Rufus's face screwed up into a grimace and he reeled away holding his very hurt hand. "That wasn't a very good idea Rufus" called Grandad after him, who then had to duck down rather sharpish as a stone sword nearly removed his head from his shoulders.

Liu Chung and Mr Yamamoto now dived into the fray jumping and kicking in true karate style at their assailants. However, this was all to no avail as no matter how hard they kicked and punched their blows had no effect.

The group was now beginning to become cornered and their only means of escape seemed to be up a flight of steps behind them. "Quick up the steps everyone" shouted Grandad and holding his stick aloft which lit up the stairway passage and urged everyone to follow him. No one needed a second invitation and they all scurried up the stairs after him.

The stairs corkscrewed upwards and upwards and seemed to be going on forever as the legs of Grandad and the rest of them got wearier and wearier and the sound of their pursuers got nearer and nearer. Rufus stopped at some point and shouted to the rest "Keep going while I try to buy us some time." Grandad came down to Rufus to try and find out what he had in mind. Rufus had taken out a length of rope from his pack and was busy making a lasso of some sort from it. He then whirled the rope above his head and hurled it upwards towards a stone feature which was sticking out from the wall some way above their heads.

The rope caught first time and Rufus pulled down hard on the rope to make it secure. "What's the plan Rufus?" asked Grandad

"Indian rope trick" replied Rufus.

"What's that?" said Grandad.

"Oh! You know, the one where the guy climbs to the top of the rope and then disappears"

Grandad looked puzzled for second before saying "And then what?" Rufus turned to Grandad and said.

"Well, all the stone 'creeps' that are trying to kill us will see me climb the rope, get to the top and disappear. Then they will all stop chasing the rest of you to try and figure out how, in the world did he do that."

Grandad knew that Rufus was joking as a wide grin grew across his face. Sometimes when people are facing danger or adversity they try to make light of the situation in order to cope with the situation. This is a common trait among soldiers, especially the more experienced and older among them and this was exactly what

Grandad, Rufus and the others were demonstrating by being 'jokey' with each other.

"This, I must see" said Grandad "Now what are you really going to do."

"Ok, you hold on to this part of the rope" said Rufus and handed Grandad a section of the rope. "I will then hold this part of the rope like this and then we walk up the stairs." The two friends then walked up the stairs until their arms was fully outstretched and then stopped. They then turned and faced down the stairs. "Now what?" asked Grandad.

"We wait a little while," said Rufus.

The sound of stone footsteps was getting louder and louder until they both could clearly see the bright, evil red eyes of the two leading stone warriors closely followed by the rest of them.

Rufus and Grandad now turned to each other. "Ready?" asked Rufus

"Aye." Replied Grandad. Rufus now yelled out "GERONIMO" and Grandad let out a highland yell as the two of them swung out on the rope as they dived through the darkness feet first hurtling towards the advancing menace.

Rufus's feet found their target first as being taller than Grandad this was only to be expected. The impact caught the leading stone warrior full in the face propelling him backwards and smashing the back of his head fully into the face of the second stone warrior who was following closely behind. This had the effect of completely removing the head of the second warrior as it too was flung backwards and smashed into the third warrior behind it Grandad's feet hit their target a split second after Rufus's with no less an effect. However, Grandad's feet being lower down than Rufus's caught the stone warrior low in the midriff. This had the effect of lifting it bodily through the air before it too smashed against the following ranks of stone, scattering stone heads and limbs all down the stairway.

Grandad and Rufus picked themselves out of the rubble and looked all about them. "Did we get them all?" asked Rufus.

"I'm not too sure," replied Grandad who then held aloft his stick and lit up the area to see.

There was broken stone heads and arms and bodies strewn all down the stairs but among the rubble others who were not dead or so badly injured were moving and trying to get up to continue the pursuit.

"Come on, let's quit while we're ahead" said Rufus as the pair of them once more ran on up the stairs to catch the others up.

They had not gone far before they reached the top of the stairs, which then led through a large open area with a doorway away to the right hand side. Grandad led the way forward with Rufus following close behind heading straight for the doorway. As they approached the doorway and ran through a voice yelled "NOW"

Grandad's legs were suddenly tripped up by something and he plunged forward hitting the ground hard closely followed by six feet two inches and weighing over two hundred pounds of prime Texan cowboy. Rufus landed full square upon Grandad's back completely flattening the small Scotsman and knocking every last once of breath from his skinny body. A Japanese body immediately followed this and then a slightly smaller Chinese body all piled on top of him. This would have been topped off by an Indian body, but for Mrs Bhattacharya checking herself at the very last second and seeing that it was Grandad and Rufus and not the stone warriors who were coming after them.

It was fully five minutes before Grandad could utter his first sentence after being helped to his feet, which was, in a slow and somewhat slurred speech. "Did anyone get the number of that bus?" he inquired looking very dazed and confused.

The comrades set off once more into the gloom with Mr Yamamoto and Scamp out in front leading the way. The passage in which they were going led to a larger hall area with three passages leading off from it, two of which led down and the third which led up a flight of steps. "Which way?" said Mr Yamamoto.

"No idea" said Rufus

"I think we should be trying to get back down" said Mrs Bhattacharya, "after all, that's where Jamie was." This was agreed by all but which of the two stairways should they choose. Mr Yamamoto then suggested that it might be wiser to send someone ahead to see where the stairs led. This was also agreed. So Yamamoto and Liu Chung set off down the first passage while the others waited.

They had not been gone long before they returned. "That was quick," said Grandad

"The stairs are completely blocked by fallen rocks and debris," replied Liu Chung.

"Well I guess that leaves only one other way down," said Rufus.

"Aye, well let's get going then," said Grandad who by now seemed fully recovered from his fall of a few minutes earlier and plunged down the second leading set of stairs. The rest of them followed but Liu Chung, who was bringing up the rear paused for a second and looked back as he thought that he heard the faint sound of distant footsteps.

The stairs led to a large room and the companions spilled into it as they left the stairs. Flashing torches all around, they spotted another doorway leading out at the other side of the room. They all began to run towards it when Mrs Bhattacharya stopped and shouted, "STOP."

The Group all came slithering and sliding to a halt on the stone floor but not before Mr Yamamoto, who was leading at the time, took one step to many, and promptly plummeted down into the blackness as though a giant invisible hand had snatched him.

The rest of them peered gingerly over the edge of the black seemingly bottomless pit to try and see where Mr Yamamoto was. He was then spotted by Liu Chung's torch beam. Mr Yamamoto was hanging on to a small ledge some twelve metres down.

Grandad put his stick in the air and the whole room was lit up. Now they could see what it was that Mrs Bhattacharya's warning was about. Across the whole of the room floor there was a gaping chasm about three metres wide and goodness knows how far down it went. However, there Mr Yamamoto was, clinging on to this small ledge for his dear life.

"Hang on, we'll soon have you up," shouted Rufus to Mr Yamamoto. The team quickly got out the ropes from their packs and one end was thrown down to him. "Sorry, I can't let go of this ledge" Mr Yamamoto called up to them. "OK, don't worry" called Rufus back "we'll get someone down to "ya". A second rope was tied around Grandads waist and he was lowered down to where Mr Yamamoto clung. Grandad then tied the end of the first rope around Mr Yamamoto's waist. "There ye go son, soon have ye back upstairs" said Grandad to Mr Yamamoto.

Grandad then started to be hoisted back up to the top of the floor. When he reached the top he untied the rope from around his waist and then gave the others a lift pulling up Mr Yamamoto. It was a very grateful Mr Yamamoto who thanked everyone for his rescue when they pulled him up out of the chasm. However, just as he had finished thanking everyone his smiles turned to a look of horror, as Mr Yamamoto looked behind them to see four pairs of burning red eyes which had just entered the doorway behind them. "Look" he called out, pointing behind them.

They were trapped. A yawning black chasm in front of them and four mean, evil eyed stone warriors behind them, no doubt bent on avenging their brothers deaths on the stairs some minutes before.

"Now what'll we do?" said Rufus.

"We're open to suggestions," answered Grandad.

Then Mr Yamamoto spoke up "Keep them busy for a few minutes while I rig something up" Mr Yamamoto then whipped off his pack and began frantically undoing the straps. The others then walked slowly towards the now advancing red eyed menace.

As they got to within a few paces of each other one of the stone warriors suddenly lunged at Mrs Bhattacharya with his sword, in a move that in its speed and accuracy would have skewered a lesser being. However, with a couple of swift nimble steps that a ballerina would be proud of she avoided the oncoming stab with ease and skipped away trying to lead her attacker further away from Mr Yamamoto.

Liu Chung was busy ducking and weaving from the attention of two of the warriors while Grandad and Rufus with one end each of the same piece of rope was carefully trying to wrap the rope around another warrior's legs to try and trip him up but were not having much success, having to dodge and dive out of the warriors constant thrusts and slashes. Scamp also was trying to do his bit by attempting to bite the ankles of the stone men but not making much impression.

"You go left and I'll go right," yelled Rufus to Grandad

"Right" answered Grandad

"No...left" shouted Rufus

"Right"! Shouted Grandad.

"I SAID LEFT! Screamed Rufus

"OK THEN! Screamed Grandad, back at him. The two then scurried off in a wide circle in opposite direction around the warrior with the rope now completely wrapped around his feet. The warrior was trying to move but could only shuffle his feet a few inches. He then raised his sword to slash at the rope and severe it when Grandad yelled "NOW." Both Grandad and Rufus then pulled on the rope as hard and as fast as they could. The effect of this was to sweep the stone figure completely off his feet a full metre in the air before landing face first and breaking into tens of pieces.

"YESS! ONE NIL" shouted Grandad.

"Surely the score is now seven nil" answered Rufus

"Oh Aye, but you should not count the others as it was a different play" answered Grandad.

"Yes, but it is all part of the same game said Rufus"

"No it is not," Grandad then said.

"Of course it is" replied Rufus.

"Isnae' said Grandad.

"It is too" said Rufus.

The two of them prepared to square up to each other before they heard a loud cry and looked around just in time to see Liu Chung trip up over a piece of stone and land heavily with two warriors bearing quickly down on him.

Rufus and Grandad stopped their quarrel immediately and dashed to Liu Chung's assistance. Rufus threw himself at the warrior that was closest to Liu Chung and hit the thing square on, right in the back. This propelled the fiendish thing forward and smashed it into the wall severing its head, snapping its sword and breaking the body in half. Grandad meanwhile had distracted the other stone warrior away from Liu Chung, who by this time had picked himself off the floor and was already scurrying away to assist Mrs Bhattacharya.

While all this was happening, Mr Yamamoto had taken from his pack a small crossbow contraption and was busy rigging a line to the bolt. After he had finished attaching various slings and pulley wheels etc. he then aimed and fired the bolt from the crossbow into the ceiling at a point which was just over halfway across the chasm. He then pulled on the thin line that was attached to the bolt and was thus able to feed a thicker rope up to the pulley wheel and then back down to him.

"OK guys, Lets go" shouted Mr Yamamoto waving and flashing his torch at the others. Mrs Bhattacharya was the first to arrive. Mr Yamamoto handed her the rope and said, "Swing over."

"Is it safe?" she inquired.

"Don't know, no time to test, please, just go" Mrs Bhattacharya called for Scamp who came almost immediately and she picked him up with one hand, hesitated for just a fraction of a second before pulling on the rope and diving out into the blackness. She landed perfectly on the other side with both feet and promptly sent the rope back to Mr Yamamoto who then handed it straight to Liu Chung "Next" said Mr Yamamoto. Liu

Chung took the rope and swung swiftly across, landed and again swung the rope back to Mr Yamamoto.

Grandad and Rufus were still giving the stone warriors the run-around but were now beginning to tire a little as a couple of times they were almost caught by the swings of very sharp stone swords. "MAC, COME ON, QUICK" Shouted Mr Yamamoto. Grandad looked back at Mr Yamamoto and shouted back "YOU GO, I CANT LEAVE RUFUS JUST YET!"

Mr Yamamoto did as he was told and swung across the void to the other side but he held on to the rope. A few seconds later Grandad's shape came running out of the darkness on the other side of the chasm and with exact timing Mr Yamamoto threw out the rope to the outstretched hands of Grandad who then dove out over the black yawning chasm below him and landed with a crash on top of Liu Chung, panting and gasping.
Mr Yamamoto quickly caught the end of the rope and was ready to throw the rope back across to Rufus. However, Rufus had not arrived yet. There was concern about his non arrival among the others as they waited and waited. They could see glimpses of red flashing eyes and heard running and scuffling in the blackness. An occasional grunt and shout from Rufus who seemed to get nearer and then go further back again. All the others were now standing and calling out to Rufus. Then they heard the unmistakable sound of running oncoming feet and a big Voice boomed out "COMING THROUGH! Again with expert timing Mr Yamamoto, threw out the rope. The rope had not reached the other side before it was met with two huge, diving Texan hands grasped it and hauled his huge body behind them out over the bottomless pit. Not a split second after Rufus and only a few feet behind him came two lunging figures, swords held aloft ready to cleave Rufus in two before they ran out of ground and plummeted down into the black pit. As Rufus neared the safety of the other side he suddenly felt the bolt that anchored the rope in the roof give out under the tremendous load that it was under and before he knew it he was clawing and scratching for the other side.

Rufus landed short. He could feel himself losing his grip and was sliding backwards down the pit when suddenly four pairs of hands gripped his arms, collar, belt, and a few other unmentionable places and dragged him back up to safety.

Rufus got up, turned and went to the edge of the chasm and took a long look down into the blackness.

"I wouldn't' bother with those last two laddie, I don't think they'll be troubling us again" laughed Grandad.

"Let's hope your right," replied Rufus.

The group took up their belongings once more and headed out of the door, where they came across a small landing area with stairs going up and down. They took the downward stairs which, after a few moments led them to yet another room.

As they entered this room they were surprised to find that a strange eyrie light was coming from the other side and entered the room through a series of windows.

They all stopped and looked at each other. Mr Yamamoto signalled to the rest to be quiet and still and they did, while he undid his pack and silently crept towards the strange light.

As he got nearer the light Mr Yamamoto could hear voices and he was now very nearly on all fours as he approached the nearest window. He was just below the window. His heart was beating very fast and tiny droplets of sweat appeared on his brow as slowly, inch by inch, he raised himself up to the window ledge. He could now see that the light was coming from a dome shaped room and could make out the remnants of carvings in the ceiling. He slowly raised himself to his full height and peered very cautiously down into the room below. The sight below him very nearly took his breath away. For there, before him, not more than a few metres away, was the stone.

Mr Yamamoto had almost forgotten how beautiful it was. He had only seen it for a few minutes previously and it had changed somehow. It had grown. Not in the physical sense but like a plant when it opens its buds to reveal a beautiful flower. How it now shimmied and glowed. Its light played with your eyes, delighted and held them. Its shape was just perfect and the colours were pale and subtle, yet, very, very beautiful. He wanted to reach out and grab it and hold it to his heart, to caress it and never let it go.

However, some movement below the stone snapped him out of his spell and he now peered beyond the stone and down into the bottom of the room, where, there lay the enormous and magnificent body of the dragon which seemed to fill most of the room as it snaked its way around. Mr Yamamoto looked closer and leaned out slightly until he could see Jamie who was sat on a step with his hands clasped about his knees looking at and seemingly listening intently to the Dragon.
After a few seconds Mr Yamamoto ducked back down beneath the window and slowly and carefully made his way back to the rest of the group.

Upon his arrival back he signalled to everyone not to talk and to follow him back the way that they had come. Everyone duly followed. When they were back on the stairs, Mr Yamamoto spoke in very hushed tones about what he had seen. They then held a small whispered discussion about what to do next. It was then agreed for them all to sneak back, take a look, and then decide on tactics as to who snatches the stone, who should try and distract Grimfell and who rescues Jamie all in one fell swoop.

Some semblance of a plan was made and one by one they all crept up to the window and slowly raised their heads up above the opening. As they did so they came face to face with another head which peered in at them from the other side. They all froze in terror as the enormous head of Grimfell appeared right in front of them. "Ahh! More guests, do come in and join the party," said the Dragon.

- CHAPTER EIGHT -

DRAGON RIDE

Grandad was the first to react. He raised his stick and with the pointed end he drove it into the Dragons huge eye and at the same time fired off one of the sticks blue electrical charges. Grimfell let out a tremendous roar, which shook the whole mountain and dropped down back to the floor of the domed room.

Jamie thought that this might be a good time to leave and ran out of the room and tried to run away as fast as he could along the main hallway and into the gloom.

Grimfell soon recovered though and as quick as a flash he grabbed hold of Jamie with one of his huge claws and then sprang up the walls of the domed room back to where the rescue team had been and then took a deep breath and opened his mouth. A roaring great flame came out of it and totally engulfed the window area and all the room that lay beyond. The dragon did this for fully two minutes before stopping and looking through the windows to see if he could see if anything remained of the rescuers. He then dropped down and brought his face close to Jamie's. The stench that came from the dragon's mouth was almost unbearable and had Jamie recoiling from it. The Great mouth then opened wide and slowly Jamie was being put inside the gaping hole. Jamie's head and body was halfway inside. Jamie was kicking and screaming and hitting out with the one arm that was free and then suddenly Jamie was thrussed out of Grimfell's mouth and thrown half way across the room. He skidded across the dusty floor and came to a stop only when he crashed against the wall leaving Jamie all in a daze.

"No, not yet" said Grimfell. ""You may have some use later."

Jamie was completely stunned by this action and it took a couple of minutes before he got his senses together.

"Your friends came by but they left in hurry. I'm not sure that I got any of them but I will."

"What will you do with them?" asked Jamie.

"Do...I shall have to kill them of course," replied Grimfell. This sent shiver down Jamie's spine. It was the matter of fact way and also that Jamie knew that this was no idle threat that shocked him. Jamie knew that Grandad and the others were in grave danger.

"Don't you think it might be wiser to talk to them?" asked Jamie.

The dragon looked at Jamie with a puzzled look. "Why?" he replied.

"You need to know why they want you. They only want to protect you. It would be better if you talked to them."

"I know why they have come here. They have come to take my future and put me back into captivity. What is there to talk about?"

"Well would you let them go if they promise to leave you alone?" asked Jamie.

"They will never leave me alone, its kill or die a long, lingering, slow death. You are a child. You know nothing of your world yet," said Grimfell.

Jamie fell silent. I need to do something he thought.

Jamie sat deep in thought for a few minutes. He found it hard to swallow because his throat was very dry. He tried to clear his throat but was finding it difficult and was beginning to make gagging noises. Grimfell looked at Jamie "what's the matter?" he asked.

"Thirsty" Jamie managed to croak.

"Ah come with me," ordered the dragon. He led Jamie into the next room and pointed to a face on the wall with an open mouth. Below the face was a circular stone bowl which projected out the wall. Jamie could see that it was once a fountain but was now completely dry and had not seen a drop of water for hundreds if not thousands of years.

Jamie looked at the fountain "nice" he said.

"Oh I'm sorry," said Grimfell "here let me fix it for you." He then looked at the fountain and closed his eyes. Nothing happened for a few seconds until there came the unmistakeable sound of running water. It slowly trickled out of the mouth of the face and into the stone bowl. The trickle soon turned into a gush and was soon splashing over the sides of the bowl. "How's that?" asked Grimfell.

"Amazing" said Jamie and went to drink the water. Jamie was just going to rinse his mouth and spit it out but, the water tasted so sweet and cool that Jamie could not help but drink deep and long by putting his mouth and face into the gushing water.

"Had enough?" asked Grimfell.

"Yes thank you" replied Jamie.

"Good, I like to look after my guests," said Grimfell "However, I do have things to attend to and will have to leave you shortly to deal with the other guests"

Jamie tried to think of some to do to stop the dragon or at least give the rest of them some more time to make good their escape.

"Tell me some more about you and your kind?" said Jamie.

"No" came back the curt reply.

"Please" Jamie said.

"You will stay here and be a good boy while I go and deal with your friends," ordered the dragon. He gave Jamie a fearful stare and Jamie backed off. The stare stuck in Jamie's mind and jolted him backwards. The dragon turned began to walk away when Jamie snapped out of his fear and cried "NO" and ran up to the dragon jumped upon its back until he reached the back of its head, grabbed hold of its horns and tried to twist its head round. Grimfell was surprised at this and stood still in its tracks. "You have courage little one" said Grimfell and with a shake of his head sent Jamie flying backwards until he landed in a heap on the floor. Grimfell swung his head round and said, "No man is a match for me Jamie, now take heed." He walked off into the gloom with a growling sound coming from within his throat.

Jamie picked himself up and set off in pursuit of Grimfell and very quickly caught him up. He tried to grab hold of the monsters tail but it was too hard to keep hold of so he leapt up upon its back and jumped up and down a few times and shouting "No No No. You leave my Grandad alone you monster" Grimfell roared and set off at a gallop, deeper into the darkness with Jamie clinging on for dear life.

On they sped through the gloom, the dragon cursing as they went through corridors and up stairs and then down again. Jamie's head was swimming with all the twisting and turning and bumping up and down. Jamie's fingers were numb with pain as he tried to hold on to the dragon's scaly back. Suddenly they came to a grinding stop and the dragon span around and Jamie came slithering off the dragons back and skidded across the floor and stopped just a few inches from the fountain where they started some minutes ago but it felt a lot longer.

Jamie staggered to his feet and holding on to the rim of the bowl of the fountain he dipped his head into the water which was still pouring from the mouth of the face on the wall. He then slowly turned to face Grimfell, the water still dripping down his now very red face. But the determination still burned in his eyes. The dragon just glared at him. Jamie sensed he was about to do something and he tensed up inside. Suddenly the monster twisted and spun his tail. Jamie ducked just in time as the huge tail came hurtling toward him. The last metre of tail missed him by millimetres as it smashed clean through the fountain and straight through the wall creating a huge hole with water and shattered rock bursting out. Jamie wasted no time in getting out as he sped on all fours out of the room and then scrambling on to two feet fled for his life along the Main hallway, he could hear the dragon howling with laughter behind him as did the whole mountain.

- CHAPTER NINE -

THE STONE

After Grandad had stabbed the Dragon in the eye Liu Chung shouted "RUN" and then turned and dashed off with the rest of them closely behind. They reached the stairs and Grandad and Rufus stopped and pressed themselves against the walls. However, Liu Chung called back to them "No don't stop, it's still not safe yet. Hurry please." So Grandad and Rufus ran up the stairs behind him. They had only gone a short way when a searing blast of heat and flame came roaring up the stairway behind them and set fire to Grandad's kilt. Despite their predicament this caused some amusement to the others to see a skinny little Scotsman with his kilt on fire go flying passed them, whilst at the same time trying to pat the flames out with his hands.

They carried on going up and up, flight after flight of stairs, for what seemed ages until they came to a sudden dead end.

"Now what do we do?" gasped Rufus. No one answered straight away as, they were all too busy puffing and panting from their exertions up the stairs. "We've got to go back to help Jamie and get the stone" said Grandad after a little while. Mrs Bhattacharya agreed "But please may I rest awhile" Grandad and the others agreed. Liu Chung began to examine the blank wall in front of them and began to run his hands over the smooth surface of the stone. "I don't get it," he then said to no one in particular.

"Get what?" asked Rufus

"Well... why build a staircase to nowhere... it doesn't make sense. The people who built this place were very clever, but this just doesn't add up," replied Liu Chung.

"So what are you thinking?" asked Rufus.

Liu Chung replied "maybe a hidden door, or something?"
The others picked themselves up at the prospect
They all began to search along the walls for cracks. Rufus thought he could see something in the wall above his head and stood on a small piece of stone that was sticking out of the wall at floor level to get a better look. The stone sunk down under his weight and the whole of the blank wall in front of them swung out and up, like a big garage door.

They blinked at the sunlight which now streamed in their faces from the opening that was before them. They were on a small rocky terrace high up on the side of the mountain with beautiful views for miles and miles. They breathed deeply the cool fresh air that a slight breeze brought to them, their spirits began to rise, and they felt a lot better.

"Well...looks like I found us a way out of Dragonville" said Rufus.

"It was a complete fluke mon," laughed Grandad.

"It was not," replied Rufus.

"It was too" said Grandad. "All ye did was to put yon great clumsy feet on a bit o stone by accident"

Rufus replied, "It took great skill to put my feet exactly on the right part of the stone you ungrateful old goat."

Grandad's eyes narrowed as he squared up to Rufus. " Old goat is it... well put 'em' up, you big barrel o lard"

Grandad and Rufus each took up a boxing stance and began to dance around making threatening gestures and sounds before being pulled apart by the others.

Jamie was by now quite exhausted after blundering about in the dark and decided to rest for a while. He noticed that the floor was beginning to slope upwards and could just make out a rather large opening some way ahead. He walked ahead but stopped momentarily to listen. He could hear a roaring sound which was getting loader and louder by the second. Jamie decided that it could only be one thing, the Dragon. He looked around for somewhere to hide. He saw an opening to his left and darted in to it. He had only gone a few paces when he tumbled down a set of steps, hit his head against the wall, and became unconscious.

Jamie had no idea how long he was out for. All he knew was that his head hurt, he had grazed both knees and an elbow, which was smarting. He gingerly picked himself up and slowly felt his way back up the stairs from which he had tumbled. He reached the main hallway again and cautiously peered all around. He listened. All was silent now and there was no sign of the dragon. He slowly walked to the middle of the hallway. He walked a few paces toward the large opening that he saw earlier but then stopped. What about the stone, thought Jamie. I must try and get it back. And without any more thought on the matter Jamie headed back down the hallway towards the Stone.

The transformation from an ordinary little boy into an audacious, brave, and daring young man was almost complete. His spirit of adventure had won through and now he boldly walked back into danger. However, Jamie was not reckless. He proceeded with great caution, keeping close to the side where there were other openings and keeping mental notes of possible escape routes and 'hidey holes' stopping every now and again behind fallen debris to listen and peer both ahead and behind.

The glow from the stone grew brighter as Jamie got nearer. He stopped again and listened intently for the slightest of sounds. There were none except for the very loud beating of Jamie's heart which he felt sure the Dragon could hear if he was around. He crept silently up to the large domed area keeping as close to the wall as possible and slowly put his head round the corner to see. All seemed well neither sight nor sound of Grimfell as Jamie crept further out toward the middle of the larger domed area, all the time keeping a wary eye on the smaller room from where the light was coming.

Jamie could now see right into the smaller domed room and he now slowly advanced towards it. Once again the beautiful light bathed Jamie in its splendid colours. His head stopped aching and he forgot about his cuts and grazes as he looked up at the wonderful glow. He stood there for a full minute, just looking and admiring before he pulled himself out of his trance. "Now how do I get it down from there?" Jamie wondered and then began to look around for things to try and build into a set of steps so that he could reach it. He searched around and collected bits of rubble and debris and began to build a set of crude steps against the pillar right under the floating stone. The idea was to build them high enough to climb up and then grab the stone and be off before the Dragon came back.

This was proving more difficult than Jamie had thought. Not only was it taking a long time to search for suitable building materials, but also when he built it, the structure would not hold his weight and he would come crashing down after he had put no more than a few steps together. He would just have to think of a better way to get the stone down.

In his frustration Jamie sat down and picked up a stone and threw it against the wall. He carried on throwing stones for a couple of minutes until he threw one right up in the air. It hit the wall and came down causing Jamie to duck out of the way very quickly. That gave Jamie an idea. "What if I throw a stone high enough to land on top of the stone and perhaps bring it down," he thought. But what if you break the stone by hitting it too hard thought Jamie again. I need something to throw that will bring it down but not harm it, but what?

Jamie thought for a little while and then came up with the idea of putting stones inside of his sweatshirt sleeves and tying knots at the cuffs using his laces to tie stones into the waist. He could then use the sweatshirt to throw over the stone and perhaps bring the thing down. This Jamie did. He worked as fast as he could and in a few short moments he was ready for his first attempt. It failed miserably. So did the second, third, fourth, fifth and sixth. He was improving his aim though, he was now only missing by half a metre instead of the usual full one, and he was succeeding in getting the sweatshirt to open out like a parachute when it came down instead of like a wet rag.

Eventually, after many attempts Jamie finally succeeded. The sweatshirt enveloped the stone and as it descended it plunged the whole room into total blackness for a split second until its light found gaps underneath its shroud and its golden light spilled out from beneath and shone on the ground.

What happened next took Jamie by surprise, instead of the stone plummeting down and hitting the ground it just hung in the air and only after a few seconds started to descend, very slowly.

When it had reached head height Jamie took hold of his sweatshirt and pulled it down to his chest. He slowly and deliberately pulled it off but, not before he had reached underneath and took a firm grip on the stone, it was beautifully smooth and warm to the touch and it did have a slight weight but it was hard to fathom out. This was because it floated in the air but Jamie found it easy to move and could carry it easily. He then wrapped up the stone in his sweatshirt leaving just enough light to act as a guide through the tunnels as Jamie set off to find a way out.

- CHAPTER TEN -

CORNERED

Grimfell was madder than a mad thing. After searching many of the hallways and corridors he decided that they must have escaped to the outside of the mountain. He sped down the main hallway like a runaway express train, roaring and cursing and vowing vengeance against his enemies, especially to the little one who had poked him in the eye. "I'll teach him to poke me in the eye. I'll squeeze him until his eyes pop out. I'll roast him and melt him, stamp him and belt him, bite him and chew him, kill him and do him."

In his rage, the dragon had forgotten about Jamie as he flew off out of the secret main entrance to the underground lair and flew off to find Grandad and the rest of the rescuers. He soared into the sky and turned to the right to scour the side of the mountain where he guessed that the entrance that the rescuers took would bring them out.

He had guessed right. There they where, up ahead of him sunning themselves on a bit of a rocky ledge near to a small exit tunnel. Grimfell made a mental note to remember to smash that particular entrance after he had finished with these troublesome humans and seek out and close permanently any others that he found.

The dragon decided to approach them from out of the sun, to surprise them and thus ensure their capture and ultimate doom.

His plan worked a treat. He came screaming down and was on the rescuers before any of them saw or heard a thing. He landed like a huge bird of prey at the back of the small terrace and there was a tremendous thump as Grimfell's massive claws embedded themselves into the side of the mountain causing the ground to shake and some rocks to move and slide down the mountain.

The rescuers were just dumbstruck at the speed and suddenness of the attack and were taken completely by surprise. It must have been at least a couple of seconds before someone attempted to get back inside the tunnel. However, before two steps were taken Grimfell whipped around his huge tail and brought it smashing down on the tunnel door slamming it shut and bringing down all about it tons of rock and other matter.

He glared at his enemies, "It's not very polite to run out on your host" said Grimfell.

The rescuers backed off to the edge of terrace all huddled together for protection. Mr Yamamoto peered over the edge "It's a long way down guys," he said.

Grandad then turned and said to the Dragon "What have ye done with Jamie?" The question seemed to take the dragon by surprise as he suddenly realised that he had completely forgotten all about the young man child.

"Oh He's quite safe... for the moment," replied the dragon who then narrowed his eyes as he remembered who the questioner was. Ahh! The eye poker thought Grimfell and seemed to flare his nostrils to breathe in a big deep breath. Liu Chung then stepped forward.

"Grimfell, you have been a very naughty monkey. And, I have come to take you back home" he shouted at him. The dragon seemed to relax slightly as Liu Chung made his defiant call.

"This is my home," replied Grimfell in a low menacing voice. "I will never go back to that miserable prison that you held me in. This is my mountain, my land, and you are going to pay for all those years that you and your fellow humans tortured me. It's payback time Liu Chung and I'm going to start with.....YOU." At this the dragon pounced upon Grandad. Snatching him with one of his huge front claws and pinning him to the ground.

Grandad could feel the huge weight of the creature that held him and was slowly squeezing the life out of his thin bony body. He kicked and squirmed and wriggled, cursed and swore but it was no use. The rest of the rescuers came rushing to Grandads aid and tried to force open the gigantic claw. They pulled and tugged and pushed and shoved with all their might. But they could not move the claw a millimetre. A hundred of the world's strongest men would not have broken the dragons grip or indeed moved it by so much as a millimetre.

Suddenly a voice spoke inside Grimfell's head, a voice so soft and gentle and beautiful that the dragon suddenly stopped thinking about squeezing the life out of the miserable little maggot it had in his claw and even lessened his grip slightly.

The voice belonged to Mrs Bhattacharya of course and she was pleading with the dragon not to harm Grandad. "Dear, sweet, wonderful, calamitous, disastrous Grimfell." Began Mrs Bhattacharya (If anyone else had called a dragon Dear, sweet or wonderful this would have infuriated the thing and would probably cost him or her their lives) "could you please stop what you are doing and spare the life of this poor worthless wretch, for to kill him now quickly would not give you any satisfaction later. You must first punish him, to teach him a lesson and his companions too. You must threaten, frighten, and torture him until he begs to be killed. You must think up lots of wicked ways to hurt him and his friends so that all humans will fear and dread you and once again dragons will rule the earth."

This last piece of guidance seemed to strike accord with the dragon and his eyes seemed to mist over as he mused over the thought. Suddenly there appeared a great golden flash that streaked from out of the sky and stopped dead in the air just a few metres out from the area in which they all stood. It was the rocket ship that had brought them to the mountain. The pilot had indeed escaped from the rock fall at the entrance to the old mine and had somehow managed to get to the rocket ship and had taken off and been scouring the outside of the mountain for signs of their reappearance. The pilot had spotted the dragon flying to this spot on the mountain and had decided to investigate.

Grimfell suddenly snapped out of his daydream and his eyes blazed red his nostrils flared and chest swelled up as he took a deep breath. Liu Chung waved frantically at the pilot to go as just in time the pilot kicked in the engine and shot off again into the sky.

This action proved to save the pilots life as a split second later would have seen the rocket ship engulfed in flames as Grimfell breathed a huge sheet of white hot flames toward him. Seeing the rocket escape his deadly breath enraged the dragon and he let out a deafening roar as he snatched hold of Liu Chung with his other free front claw and leaped off the ledge in hot pursuit of the fleeing rocket.

The rocket however, did not totally escape without damage. The rear exhaust ports were caught in the dragons fierce blast and the damage was effecting the engines to such an extent that the rocket could not go very fast.

Grimfell was gaining rapidly upon the stricken aircraft and spat an enormous fiery ball at it. The pilot just managed to dodge the deadly venom and was taking evasive manoeuvres to try and shake off the dragon which was closing in from behind spraying more fire at the rocket.

The rest of the rescue team felt helpless and could only watch as the rocket did all kinds of aerial acrobatics to try and avoid its pursuer. However, it was only a matter of time before the dragon finally caught the limping rocket, and with a quick 'whip' of his huge tail he completely sliced the tail section of the rocket off from the main fuselage. The rocket was then sent spiralling downward carrying its pilot to his doom.

Grimfell followed the rocket for a few seconds and when he seemed satisfied that the rocket would not pull out of its death dive he returned to the mountain ledge. The rescuers were staring in disbelief as they followed the trail of smoke from the damaged rocket down into the densely forested valley far below them.

Grimfell returned to the mountain and the others.

All the years of being held in captivity, unable to exercise properly, combined with the long flight from China and Japan. Plus all his other exertions in such a small space of time had all taken their toll on Grimfell and his chest was heaving from the effort, trying to draw in great gulps of air his long tongue was hanging out and heavy great gloop's of saliva dripped from his huge mouth and his eyes looked very glazed. His grip on his two prisoners slackened and although Grandad and Liu Chung were very dizzy from being flipped every which way they, both managed to squeeze themselves free from the dragon's great claws, but, because the dragon had held them so tightly they could only just breathe and they both just lay on the ground exhausted.

Mrs Bhattacharya was the first to run over to Grandad and try and drag him away from the dragon's claw but wasn't making much progress until Rufus arrived and lifted the limp, but still alive Grandad, away to a safer part of the ledge. Mr Yamamoto dragged Liu Chung away and laid him beside Grandad.

While Mrs Bhattacharya administered some aid to the two injured people the dragon was still huffing and puffing and making all manner of loud grunting and snorting noises while trying to get his breathe back. Liu Chung was tugging at Mr Yamamoto's shirt trying to tell him something but Liu Chung's voice was so low and sounded so croaked that Mr Yamamoto could not tell a word that he said. Finally, Liu Chung gave up trying to speak and instead just pointed to something that lay on the ground a few metres away. It was a small silver box with a hinged lid that had fallen out from Liu Chung's sleeve when Mr Yamamoto had dragged him away from the dragon's claw. Liu Chung gestured that he wanted Mr Yamamoto to bring him the small box. Mr Yamamoto got up and advanced the few paces needed to retrieve the box, picked it up and took one pace back before the dragons huge roar stopped him dead in his tracks.
"What are you doing?" demanded Grimfell. Mr Yamamoto stopped and with his back still turned

towards the dragon replied in a rather shaky voice "Oh... n.n.nothing." The dragon took a step closer.
"Turn round and face me" said Grimfell.

Mr Yamamoto hesitated for a few seconds as suddenly he was grabbed by the collar of his shirt by the dragon's mouth and was tossed several metres in the air and came down with a huge bump.

The small silver box was sent spinning out of Mr Yamamoto's hand and went clattering along the ground between the dragon's legs. Grimfell eyed the rest of the rescue team as Mr Yamamoto lay slowly writhing on the ground. "You puny weak humans are no match for a Dragon. With one small puff of my breath I could blow you all off this mountain" he said. His speech was laboured however and his stance seemed a little wobbly.

Liu Chung managed to raise himself a little and spoke to the dragon "Grimfell, it is many hundreds of years since you last felt the wind under you. You are not well. Let me take you back with me to China where you can be well looked after and you will get fitter and be well fed. The world has changed much since you were last out. Humans now rule the earth. The time of Dragons has long gone. It is now the time of the human. If you don't come back with me they will hunt you down with terrible weapons and kill you. Please Grimfell, I beg you to stop this madness now, before it is too late and come back with me."

Almost before Liu Chung had stopped speaking the dragon let out a furious roar "NO! I will never go back. This is my mountain and my time is not over." As he spoke Grimfell lurched forward towards Liu Chung and as he did so his back claws kicked open the small silver box which was lying near his rear claws. Out of the box spilled lots of small luminous green creatures which looked like centipedes. There seemed to be thousands and millions of the little creatures as they continued to pour out of the tiny box and milled around the ground beneath the Dragons body. The centipedes scurried around the ground for a couple of seconds before they started to scamper up the rear claws of the dragon and up and on to his belly and over on to his back. The rescuers watched completely fascinated by the goings on which was unfolding before their eyes.

Grimfell was completely oblivious to what was going on beneath his fearsome body and continued to shout his defiance at Liu Chung. "You only want me to go back so that you can learn how to become wise. You want to take from me all that the Dragon knows. All our secrets you wish to know. Then you will kill me and eat my brains, just as your emperors did to some of my friends and relations. Well I'm not going back Liu Chung ...and neither are you," he added menacingly.

Grimfell stepped closer and raised his giant claw high to bring it crashing down upon Liu Chung when he noticed the luminous green tide that was sweeping up his claw and was already swarming along his flanks and up on top of his head. The Dragon stopped completely dead. He looked at Liu Chung. There was fear and surprise in the Dragons eyes as he then said, "I knew I could never trust a human." Liu Chung could only look back at Grimfell with sorrow in his eyes and say "Sorry, it was an accident. I really did want to"... The rest of the words no one heard as Grimfell felt the first of the centipedes enter his nostrils and let out a terrible roar and began to snort and buck like a wild horse that doesn't want to be ridden. He threw himself into the air and came crashing down on his back, kicking his legs and thrashing his tail about. He was like a thing possessed grunting and roaring.

Grandad and the rest had to dodge the dragon's tail as it whipped and swiped. The whole mountain seemed to shake and quiver as the dragon thrashed about, trying in vain to shake off the green swarm that had invaded it.

It was left to Rufus to state the obvious "We're gonna be swept to our deaths, less we git off this ledge real quick" he shouted. The others nodded in agreement as they cowered near the edge of the precipice.

"What do you suggest we do?" shouted Mrs Bhattacharya in reply. "We are in no fit state to climb either up or down, or have you got some wings in your pack, so we can just fly off here?"

Rufus grinned back "Fraid not Ma am. You're the only angel round here."

Their plight was very short lived however, as Grimfell charged forward, his eyes now showing a distinct yellow colour and launched himself off the ledge and took off into the evening sky.

They all watched from the ledge as Grimfell flew erratically, still clawing at his face and snout, frantically trying to scrape off the hoards of centipedes still invading his nostrils and slowly eating their way into his brain. In one last desperate manoeuvre the dragon shot straight up into the air until he was just a tiny dot in the sky. Then he just plummeted down and disappeared from view as the side of the mountain got in the way from seeing the final part of the death plunge.

- CHAPTER ELEVEN -

A WAY OUT

Jamie gazed into the beautiful stone, his gaze held hypnotically by the swirling light that emitted from within. Slowly the features of a face seemed to appear. A face that spoke but Jamie could not understand what it was saying. The face seemed to be repeating the same thing over and over until Jamie's head was swimming. He finally covered the stone over again with his sweatshirt and he began to feel better. With the stone covered all the hall went very black, so he uncovered a small section just enough to throw some light out to where he was going.

Jamie set off back up the long hallway, walking very cautiously and taking time to stop and listen every now and again. Eventually he came to the point where he had reached before, he recognized the huge opening now slowly appearing through the gloom, and he could also see that it was getting lighter. He stopped to listen. He could not hear anything so he slowly advanced further up the slight slope until he reached the top of a huge flight of steps which led down to a large entrance hall and which in turn led to a huge opening through which poured daylight.

Jamie's heart leapt at the sight of the way out. He wanted to run down the steps and leap out into the lovely fresh air and was just about to do this when he stopped. "What if this is some kind of trick," he thought to himself. Jamie then stepped slowly down the steps all the time peering ahead and listening intently to any sound. He reached the bottom step and crouched low to look up and out of the huge opening which was now only a few short metres away. There was still no sight or sound of the dragon. Jamie crept up to the entrance, his heart pounding in his chest. Two metres ahead lay freedom.

Jamie could not hold back any longer, he suddenly leapt forward shouting his head off until he was through the entrance and out into fresh air and wonderful daylight at last. However, Jamie's joy did not last long and he had to pull up very sharply before he plunged over the edge of a very long drop onto some very jagged rocks some hundred metres below.

Jamie searched desperately for a way down but it was no use, it was a straight drop all the way. The dragon had made this entrance very well. There was no way to climb down and the climb up was even more daunting, a sheer cliff face going vertically up, seemingly forever. Jamie let out a cry of frustration and kicked a small piece of rock of the edge and watched as it went straight out and then slowly curved through the air before clattering among the rocks far below.

Jamie slumped down with a heavy sigh and suddenly all the bumps and bruises that he had suffered but had forgotten about on his journey, all came back with a vengeance. His knees and elbows hurt. The bump on the head had started to ache again, his middle was chafed where the rope had cut into him to stop his fall and on top of that he was feeling very hungry all of a sudden.

The view from the tunnel entrance was quite spectacular. It faced south and in the clear blue sky Jamie could see for miles and miles. Not far away and below Jamie could see a small lake with the odd building nestling along its shoreline. There was a small river that led down from the mountain and fed the lake upon its eastern shore and also a group of fir and pine trees quite near. The whole scene looked beautiful, clean, and undisturbed. Jamie felt dirty. He wished that he could be down by the lake and swim in its lovely waters and wash some of the dirt and grime out of his hair.

Jamie began to wander whether there might be another way down and so he went back inside the tunnel and climbed back up the steps to where the main hallway was. He searched all around until he came across a small doorway, which in turn led to a narrow passage. Jamie followed the passage as it went deeper and deeper down and down into the mountain. The narrow passage now turned into a series of steps which got steadily steeper and steeper as they twisted and turned both this way and that. Jamie was determined to find out just where the steps ended and so he began to go faster and faster down the stone staircase. He was now bounding along going three steps at a time when suddenly his feet slipped upon a wet stair and he went tumbling down. The stone was flung into the air as Jamie's feet left the ground. He suddenly landed with a huge splash into dark ice cold water. He came to the surface coughing and spluttering and gasping for air and clawing for where he thought the steps should be. Then with good fortune his fingers finally touched some stone and he finally pulled himself out of the black, cold, water.

The cold water took Jamie's breath away and he stood crouched over taking short shallow breaths. His breath finally settled down and Jamie crouched on the stone steps, arms folded, teeth chattering staring at the golden light which was lighting up the depths of the water some two or three metres below the surface. Jamie realised that 'The stone' was sinking further and further down into the depths of the icy water. He realised that he must do something soon or the stone will be out of his depth. So brave Jamie dived down into the deep dark water and swam as fast as he could towards the beautiful shining light. Down and down Jamie swam until he thought he would never reach it until his outstretched hands finally grabbed it and he turned to head for the surface. As he did so Jamie thought that he saw a shaft of light which was illuminating the water some ten or perhaps some fifteen metres further along the underwater tunnel. It was sunlight, sunlight meant outside, outside meant out of here, and out of here meant escape and escape meant FREEDOM!

Jamie rushed to the surface and clambered back to the steps taking deep slow breaths of air. It was a good job he was a good swimmer thanks to his parents who had taken him to have swimming lessons from a very early age. However, swimming in a local swimming pool which was warm and bright was one thing, but swimming in an underground tunnel in freezing cold black water, and having to swim underwater also was altogether something else.

Jamie looked into the beautiful stone that he held in his cold trembling fingers and thought of his parents and Grandad who he wanted to see again. The stone seemed to emit warmth as Jamie held it and his hands stopped trembling. The warm glow ran all through his hands and into his arms. It continued into his body and down into his numbing legs until at last it ran up his spine and into his head. Jamie closed his eyes and took deep breathes, basking in the warm glow of the stone. Then Jamie tucked the stone under his left arm and dived, head first into the chilling blackness.

Down and down he went until he could see the shaft of light up ahead and he swam as fast as he could towards it. His swimming technique was good and he made good progress up to a point. But, Jamie could feel his breath beginning to fail. His heart began to pound faster and a slight panic began to set in as he kicked hard for the light. Hampered by the burden under his left arm his technique began to become ragged as he struggled to get to the light. His lungs were now beginning to feel as if they would burst if he did not reach air soon. He soon became frantic. His chest was burning with pain; his head began to swim as he tossed it to and fro. He was heading up now but was still some way off the shaft of light but he needed air. He needed to breathe. He was still kicking furiously when his head suddenly burst out of the water as he gulped and gasped in the precious air that he had unexpectedly and very gratefully found in the roof of the tunnel.

Jamie could not believe his luck there was an air gap between the roof of the tunnel and the water and Jamie breathed deeply of the stale but wonderful air. He trod water and began to get his breath back. He lifted the stone out of the water and held it aloft. The stone's light pushed back the darkness and as it did so Jamie could see that he was in a huge chamber. He could just make out a shoreline. Something was glittering in the pale light of the stone to the rear of the cave.

Jamie swam toward the side until he could feel the bottom of the cave floor rise underneath him and so he stood up and wade the rest of the way. Jamie brushed the water away from his eyes as he walked with caution toward the now gleaming and glittering pile that lay ahead of him. Jamie stopped about a metre short of the pile and bent down and picked up a small flat round shape. It was cold to the touch and surprisingly heavy for its size. It was of course a coin, a gold coin and Jamie brought it closer to his eye to examine its markings. It was beautifully made with a Kings head on one side and strange markings on the other. He put it straight into his pocket and promptly bent down to the pile to grab another handful of coins. Again the weight of the coins surprised Jamie and he let them trickle out of his hand and as they landed back on the pile they made a chinking sound. Jamie grabbed up another handful of coins and stuffed them his pocket. He then let go of the stone and of course it just stayed hovering in mid air while Jamie began frantically to stuff more and more coins into his pockets until they could hold no more and were bulging out and nearly pulling his trousers down.

Jamie began to climb up the pile. It was enormous. There must have been tens of thousands of gold and silver coins with golden goblets and dishes sticking out of the pile here and there. There were also gold chains and necklaces with all types of jewels encrusted within them. Jamie could not believe his luck. His eyes widened as he surveyed the huge mound of fantastic wealth that he had discovered and it was all his. He let out a loud yell of delight as his mind began to dream up all kinds of weird things about what he was going to do with all his money. The things he could buy. Mansion houses with swimming pools, big flash motor cars, a huge yacht, his own private jet airplane. As Jamie dreamed he frantically hung the gold necklaces around his neck and was feverously trying to stuff things inside his shirt and anywhere else they would fit. When Jamie couldn't possibly carry any more treasure, as the weight was pulling him down he staggered down to the 'Stone', plucked it out of the air and then walked slowly back towards the water.

As Jamie's feet splashed into the icy cold water he suddenly stopped, blinked his eyes a few times and then he came to his senses. "WHAT AM I DOING?" He shouted out very loudly. "THIS IS CRAZY!" Jamie then turned around walked back to the mound of treasure and removed all the gold from around his neck and threw it back onto the mound of treasure. He also emptied all his pockets. As he did so he was muttering to himself "Jamie, you nearly lost it then pal. You crazy fool you nearly got yourself drowned and all because of a few bits of shiny metal." When Jamie had put back all the gold he actually felt better, the madness had passed, and he was himself again, although he did keep just one gold coin and he slipped it back into his pocket.

Jamie collected the 'stone' and walked back into the water, before he dived again he paused and took a big deep breath and ducked once again into the dark icy depths. Once under the water he headed down until he could see the shaft of light ahead and he kicked his legs as fast as he could towards it. There were only a few metres to go now as he passed through the tunnel and into a much lighter and wider area. He could see daylight above him now and he swam upwards and eventually his head broke the surface.

Jamie had surfaced in a lake. It was the same lake that Jamie had looked down upon from the mountain tunnel entrance previously. There were quite steep rocks near to where Jamie had come up and he swam out, heading across the lake until he saw a small jetty with a small boat moored along side. He headed towards it and eventually reached it. As he stopped swimming and allowed his legs to sink down, his feet touched the gritty stony bottom of the lake and Jamie then waded to the rocky shoreline, where he slumped down on a large flat stone.

Jamie sat there and began to get his breath back. He looked around for somewhere he could find shelter. Perhaps there was someone he could ask for help. He got up and started to walk towards a small boathouse. Suddenly, Jamie became aware of a high pitched noise coming from above somewhere. It was a screaming sort of sound, low at first but getting louder all the time. Jamie's heart started to pound and panic began to set in, as he knew it was the dragon returning, but before Jamie could react something caught his eye and as he looked up he saw the dragon come plummeting out of the clear evening sky. Jamie was too weary and mesmerised to do anything but just stand and watch as the huge missile headed towards him. However, something did not look right to Jamie and although he had never seen a dragon in flight the creature did not seem in full control and seemed to be falling and not flying.

The dragon disappeared behind the huge mountain for a few seconds. Jamie blinked a few times looked behind him at the dense wood and considered making a dash into there. Suddenly there was an almighty crack like the sound of thunder and Jamie spun around back towards the mountain. The dragon had regained some measure of control and had managed to guide his body away from smashing straight into the huge mountain but not miss it completely as Grimfell hit the topmost ridge which sent him tumbling, along with hundreds of tons of rock. With an almighty splash the dragon smashed right in the middle of the small lake followed by all the tons of rock.

Jamie watched, his eyes wide and mouth open as the huge wave caused by the Dragon went wider and wider until it crashed along the lake side lifting Jamie and the small boats out of the water and sent then crashing and smashing over the rocky shore. The wave carried Jamie along some thirty metres until it deposited him among the line of fir trees, which upon one fine specimen he cracked his head and remembered no more.

CHAPTER TWELVE

RESCUED

It was several moments before anyone spoke. "Has he gone?" asked Grandad to no-one in particular. "He has gone for the moment" replied Liu Chung picking himself gingerly off the ground before adding "But I do not know for how long." The rest of the team also picked themselves and helped Grandad and Mr Yamamoto to get to their feet. "OK! Now what'll we do to try and git down" Asked Rufus. No one answered as no one had any good suggestions to make.

Mrs Bhattacharya looked out at the plume of black smoke which was coming out of the forest far below and some two or three kilometres away to their right, which was the crash site of their rocket. "I wonder if the pilot managed to get out?" she murmured to herself. She suddenly caught a small glint of a flash in the sky straight ahead and she shielded her eyes from the sun and strained to look in the direction of the flash. Yes, there it was again, and another one. There were now two distinct shiny metal objects heading in their direction and coming very fast. "LOOK"! Shouted Mrs Bhattacharya and pointed excitingly in the direction of the two shiny flying objects. "I think we are saved" The others all looked up and when they saw the two rockets they began yelling and waving their arms in delight.

The two rockets slowed right down as they approached the plume of smoke coming from the forest and began to circle. They then both hovered above the trees until one of them descended into the trees and vanished. The other one still hovered for a few minutes until it suddenly took off and headed toward the mountain.

Grandad and the rest were still frantically trying to catch the attention of the two rockets when Mr Yamamoto began rummaging in his pack. He then produced a small cylindrical object from his pack. He then held it at arm's length before turning to the others "This should do the trick" he called out. Mr Yamamoto then pulled out a small pin attached to the cylinder. There was a loud popping noise and then ....nothing. They all stared at the cylinder waiting for something to happen but nothing did.

"Oh! Very impressive" said Grandad sarcastically after a few seconds. Mr Yamamoto looked puzzled as he then began to peer closely at the thing in his hand. Suddenly, there was a second loud POP! And a bright crimson smoke exploded from the canister completely engulfing the whole party in a thick crimson acrid smoke.

No one dared to move out of the smoke for fear of falling off the ledge as the smoke made them cough and splutter and got into their eyes and made them very sore. There was also much shouting and cursing as Rufus could be heard above the clamour threatening, "Just ...cough! ...you...cough! ...wait...cough! ...get hold ...cough! ...you...cough! ...idiot"!

Finally the smoke cleared and the team were able to see again. The rocket had seen the smoke and was now hovering perfectly still, just a stride away from their position on the ledge. Some people left the rocket to help on board the still coughing, spitting and swearing rescue team. Once they were all on board, the team received medical attention in the form of cough medicine and eye drops. The team soon forgot all their grievances against Mr Yamamoto when they saw the sight of him. The smoke which had blown up into his face had turned his face and hair the most incredible bright crimson colour. His hair was also stuck straight up. He looked like a punk rocker tomato. When they all saw Mr Yamamoto everyone fell about in fits of hysterics.

On board the rocket was Mr Higginbottom who sought out Grandad and Liu Chung. "How's things going lads?" he asked

"Jamie is missing" replied Grandad "priority number one, find him."

"That we will, Mr McGregor. Don't you worry about that, but why you brought him along in the first place is an act of complete lunacy on your behalf. I have to tell you that I shall have to put a motion of no confidence in your ability to carry on as a member of the High Council once we get back to H.Q.

Grandads eyes narrowed to tiny little slits as he suddenly shot out a hand and grabbed Mr Higginbottom by the throat. "Ye nasty, horrible, wee man. I'll throw ye out o yon window before we go any further" screamed Grandad. Liu Chung and some others pulled Grandad and Mr Higginbottom apart amid shouts and threats and counter threat. When things had calmed down Mr Higginbottom asked Liu Chung about the dragon situation.

"We may never see him again," said Liu Chung sadly and quickly told to Mr Higginbottom the events leading up to the Dragons last flight.

"And what about the stone?" asked Mr Higginbottom.

"We do not know," replied Liu Chung. "The last time it was seen was inside the mountain. I don't recall seeing the Dragon have it outside, so perhaps it is still there." Then Grandad said, "Aye, and that was the last time we saw Jamie too. We need to get back into the mountain to find Jamie and the stone. "Yes... but how?" said Mrs Bhattacharya. The dragon has blocked both the entrances that we have used. We have brought some mining experts with us," said Mr Higginbottom perhaps we could blast a way back in?

The team began to discuss ways of reopening the entrance on the ledge to get back inside the mountain when Grandad suddenly said, "wait a minute, yon Dragon didn't come out the same way as we did. There must be another way in" The others quickly agreed with Grandad. "But it might be very well hidden" said Liu Chung "Dragons are masters of deception and the entrance may be very carefully concealed." Grandad thought for a moment and then said "look, if we leave a mining team here working on the ledge entrance, then we can go and look for the other entrance" The others agreed and the mining team, plus their equipment were left on the ledge to try and open the door blocked by the dragon while the others departed in the rocket to try and find the other entrance.

The pilot guided the rocket all up and down the west face of the mountain while the others all had their faces glued to the windows scouring the rock for traces of an entrance. They eventually came to the south face of the mountain and the rocket slowly descended down the steep near vertical massive slab of rock. Suddenly a cry went up "THERE, I SEE IT. IT'S A CAVE ENTRANCE!" It was Mr Yamamoto's voice. There were shouts of "where" from all sides before they all could see the gaping hole in the cliff face.

The pilot brought the rocket side on to the entrance with the door exactly lined up to the middle of the entrance. It was quickly lowered out onto the cave lip and out sprang Grandad closely followed by Rufus and the others. They rushed through the opening and up the stone stairs until they came to the hallway. The beams from their flashlights flicked this way and that searching for the best way to go.

They chose to keep together and search the most obvious place first which just happened to be the main big hallway in which they were heading. Deep into the mountain they went, striding out with a purpose, ignoring the warnings of Liu Chung that the dragon may not be dead. They eventually reached the part where the main hallway joined the antechamber and where they had first glimpsed the dragon by looking down on him from the gallery at the top. The team searched all around but found no trace of Jamie or the stone. Liu Chung found some footprints of Jamie which led out of the antechamber and back to the way they had come.

Mrs Bhattacharya heaved a big sigh and put her hands on her hips.
"What's the matter girl?" asked Grandad. Mrs Bhattacharya looked all around the huge hall and then

said, "I don't feel anything. There's nothing here alive or dead, just cold empty stone."

Grandad then asked her was she sure she replied "O yes quite sure" She then turned to face Grandad and she could see the hurt in his eyes that they had not found Jamie. "Don't worry," she said, "I'm sure we will find him soon, and he will be well."

They traced Jamie's footprints back along the hall and back to the entrance. "Any luck" Called the others, who were waiting back at the rocket.

"No" came back the forlorn answer. Suddenly a cry from inside the cave "OVERHERE" it was Rufus. Grandad and the others rushed over to him. He was crouched down looking at the ground. "Jamie's footprints, they lead to that small tunnel over there," he said. Rufus then led the way down the small tunnel closely followed by Grandad, Mrs Bhattacharya, Mr Yamamoto, and finally Liu Chung who was still insisting that they be careful.

They followed the Tunnel all through its twisty turns and steep steps until they came to an abrupt stop. "Urgh! Dead End" called out Rufus as he pulled out his wet right foot from the dark icy watery trap that was immediately in front of him. They held a quick discussion as to what to do next. "There must be another tunnel which leads off this one," said Rufus

"I did not see any," replied Mr Yamamoto.

"Nor I" said Mrs Bhattacharya.

"Aye, we must a passed the blessed thing and it's no wonder wi this great galoot leading the way" said Grandad. Referring to Rufus

"Hey! Hey! Hey! Who are you calling a galoot?" replied Rufus. I'm a better tracker than you are. I was taught to track by that great Indian scout 'Grey Owl'. I followed these here tracks all the way down to here. Thar just 'aint' no way that Jamie could have turned off .Cos if he did I would have tracked him, and when I track somebody, they stay tracked."

Grandad turned to face Rufus and said in a firm voice "You missed the turning. You must have missed it."

Rufus and Grandad then proceeded to argue until Mrs Bhattacharya intervened yet again.

They then decided to retrace their steps and see if they did indeed miss a turning. They very carefully travelled back up the steep steps and the narrow twisting passage until they arrived back at the entrance.

"See, I told 'ya' I never missed no turning," Rufus called to Grandad when he came out of the small passage.

"Aye ye were right Rufus, sorry a snapped at ye back there." Rufus could see that Grandad was becoming more and more anxious about Jamie and then said

"Aw forget it old timer. Don't worry we'll find him."

They all scrambled back on board the rocket where some light refreshments were waiting for them. Mr Higginbottom ordered the pilot to land somewhere where they could eat and decide what their next move would be. The pilot took the rocket down and landed on a flat area quite close to where the small lake was. The other rocket which had picked up the mining experts off the high ledge, seeing, as they were no longer needed to reopen that entrance, joined them very soon. There was also another person who they managed to pick up. It was the pilot of the first rocket which had brought them. He had managed to parachute out just before the dragon sliced the rocket in two and had landed safely (apart suffering from a broken collar bone, and various cuts and bruises when he crashed through the trees and was found hanging upside down dangling from a tree about a kilometre from the crash site)

Grandad and the rest of the rescue team were overjoyed when they saw he was safe and congratulated him on his skill and good fortune. Mr Yamamoto sat down on the grass before jumping up and exclaiming "Urgh why is it so wet around here?" and trying to wipe his trousers dry.

"Say, your right" replied Rufus "this whole area is really wet. Why?" Everyone now noticed the same thing and started to wonder why. They noticed the smashed wooden buildings and boats which had been washed right up to the trees and beyond. Liu Chung had noticed something too. He had noticed some strange bubbles coming up towards the middle of the lake. He suddenly began to take off his boots. Then he removed his socks and walked down to the lake. The others who wondered what he was up to watched him. Mr Higginbottom then called to him "Liu Chung, I don't think this is the right time for a paddle."

Liu Chung did not stop but merely held up his hand to signal them that he was not just going for paddle. Liu Chung then walked into the water until it was up to his waist and then swam out to where he could see the bubbles coming up. He then took a deep breath and dove down into the murky depths.

He was down for a full minute before he reappeared again and swam back to the waiting party on the lake shore. Everybody wanted to know what he had seen and was asking questions all at the same time. Liu was quite out of breath and held up his hand to stop them before saying "Grimfell" and pointing back to the lake. This caused quite a bit of commotion and Mr Higginbottom called for the pilots to start up the rockets and calling for people to hurry up and get on board. Before Liu Chung called out "No, you do not understand. He's dead... Grimfell is dead. He must have crashed straight into the lake when he fell from the sky. He must have caused a huge splash when he hit the water. That is why all around is smashed and wet."

Now they all understood. There was excited chatter and laughter among many who stood around but Liu Chung did not laugh. He was very sad. For all the damage and problems that Grimfell had caused he really loved Dragons. He blamed himself for not getting to know them better. For not keeping a tight enough vigil on his charge of keeping him safe and well. And now he had killed him. The last of the great dragons gone, forever.

Grandad and the others walked over to Liu Chung and Mrs Bhattacharya put a blanket around his shoulders. "Your sadness is great," said Mrs Bhattacharya. "You blame yourself too much. The dragon was a great spell master. He made you love him." Liu Chung turned to face Mrs Bhattacharya and then said, "I know that was my weakness. He sensed it and used it against me. I needed to be strong against him but I failed in my duty and now there are no more great dragons left and the world is now a much sadder place."

"What do you mean no great dragons left?" said Grandad with a slight sneer.

"Just what I said" replied Liu Chung "No more Dragons, all gone."

"Nonsense man why have ye never heard of 'Nessie' the 'Loch Ness Monster'?" said Grandad.

Liu Chung smiled and looked at Grandad. "Of course I have. But he is a 'water dragon' why?"

"Because," said Grandad. "Nessie is a mighty fine Dragon. And he's a very good dragon. He's a Scottish dragon. And if ye'll snap out of all this guilty feeling nonsense you have. I'll arrange for you to meet the great beastie."

Liu Chung's eyes lit up. "You are not joking with me are you Mac?" He said.

"Certainly not" replied Grandad. At that Liu Chung flung his arms around Grandad and gave him an enormous hug.

"All right that's enough o that," said Grandad lets now get down to the serious matter of trying to find Jamie."

Mr Higginbottom called everybody round and was asking for suggestions as to how the rest of the search was to proceed. While everyone gathered around, Mrs Bhattacharya got a funny feeling and a cold shiver went through her. It would be dark soon and she began to let her thoughts focus upon Jamie. A boy all alone, frightened, hungry, probably hurt. She left the group and started to amble around the lake getting further from the crowd. The funny feeling started to get stronger as she approached the pine woods. The cold shivers got stronger and stronger and her teeth began to chatter. But she did not stop. She walked up the gradient to the edge of the woods and peered through the trees at something she saw. As she got nearer she could see something in the trees but she could not make it out because of the darkness which was now creeping through the woods and enveloping everything inside it. Mrs Bhattacharya brushed aside the lower branches of the first tree and slowly stepped into the gloom. She stopped for a few seconds to let her eyes adjust to the darkness. There a few feet away from her, lay what at first she thought was a bundle of old clothes. But, as she got closer she could make out that it was a small body. It was Jamie.

Mrs Bhattacharya quickly checked him over for signs that he was alive, and he was, but he was unconscious. She then shouted for help as loud as she could and carried on shouting until help arrived.

Help very quickly arrived, with Grandad and Liu Chung leading the way. As they carefully lifted Jamie up he was still clutching hold of his tightly wrapped sweatshirt. Liu Chung had to prise open Jamie's fingers in order to get him to release his grip upon it. As Liu Chung wrested the bundle from Jamie's grasp a chink of golden light sprang from a gap in it. Liu Chung then carefully uncovered the stone and the whole area was suddenly bathed in a beautiful golden glow. Liu Chung just stood there with a huge smile on his face holding the stone. Mr Higginbottom came over to him and said, "I take it that's the stone then." Then to every one's surprise Liu Chung burst out laughing and cried out "IT'S NOT A STONE! ...IT'S NOT A STONE! ...IT'S AN EGG! ...A DRAGONS EGG!"

They carried Jamie back to the rocket, removed his cold wet clothes, and wrapped him in blankets. Mrs Bhattacharya gave him some medicine, tended to his cuts and bruises and he soon came round (although his head still ached a bit). Grandad fussed around Jamie, as he'd never fussed around before and sure enough three bowls of hot soup and a mug of cocoa later and Jamie were nearly back to his old self.

Everyone was packing things away ready for the return flight. Mr Higginbottom was kept very busy checking that everything was 'cleaned up' By this he meant that all traces of their being a I.H.C.I.U.P involvement, needed to be removed and kept very secret. The cave entrance was quickly closed and 'sealed' by the mining experts, and so well was it done that no one would ever guess that an entrance had ever existed there at all. The remains of the wrecked rocket were removed and what remains there now where, was just a pile of burned dust.

Rufus came to see Jamie. "HI THERE, HERO!" He boomed when he came aboard the rocket where Jamie was. "Brought you a little present," he said and from around his back he produced Scamp. Jamie's eyes lit up, looked at the small dog and cried out "Scamp, you're alive," and held out his arms for him to come. Scamp jumped out of Rufus's hands and landed right into Jamie's lap Scamp then began to excitedly lick Jamie's face and bark and run around very excitedly and the two friends fussed over each other for the rest of the flight home.

During the flight home Jamie told the others about what had happened to him when he and Scamp became separated from the others, his encounter with the dragon and how he jumped on the dragons back to prevent it from coming after the others. There was a strange look of astonishment on the face of Liu Chung. "Stop" he said. "Tell me again, slowly."

"Why" asked Jamie.

"Just tell me please," Liu young said. Jamie then told of how he jumped upon Grimfell's back and how they careered along the tunnels and up and down stairs until he was eventually was thrown off. Liu Chung looked at Jamie very closely without blinking until he muttered, "Never has anyone ridden upon his back. He would never allow it, not unless he had the utmost respect and I have looked into your eyes and I believe you are telling the truth. Jamie you are very special." Liu Chung bowed as he said it.

"All hail the dragon rider," shouted Rufus and three cheers rang out among the company of friends. Jamie continued with his story of he took the stone when the dragon left. He also told them how he escaped from the mountain through the underground water tunnel and about the treasure he found there. Mr Higginbottom seemed very interested in that particular bit of the story and kept quizzing Jamie about its contents and its exact whereabouts. He also took an unhealthy interest in Jamie's coin. He would look at it with eyes that burned with desire.

Grandad and the others recounted their adventures. The encounter with the stone warriors really interested Jamie and he told the others about how the dragon brought them to life. Liu Chung told Jamie all about how he suspected that the stone was a Dragons egg but until he had actually seen it for himself he could not be sure, as he had never seen one before. Liu Chung held up the dragons egg for all to see and sure enough, inside the egg was a tiny baby dragon, all curled up with its already huge head tucked on to its chest and its long tail wrapped around it. He went to explain that even though Grimfell is dead his wisdom, knowledge, and Dragon lore would be kept alive through the baby. The new dragon would inherit all its parent's gifts.

"But would it not also inherit its parents bad bits as well?" asked Jamie

"Possibly," replied Liu Chung "But we now have the chance to have some influence upon the young dragon and teach him to use his powers for good and not for evil. Dragons can basically live forever (unless they are killed of course) and Grimfell was a very ancient dragon many, many centuries old and he would have probably learned his badness from others who would want to use the dragon's power for evil."

Mr Yamamoto wanted to know how did Grimfell know that an egg had been discovered and how did he know where to find it. Liu Chung told him that it was probably intuition. "Dragon eggs are very, very rare and they are guarded very jealously and are extremely well hidden," Liu Chung said. "When this egg was discovered he knew almost immediately where it was. He became agitated and would not rest until he had recovered it."

"Would not the egg go bad after such a long time buried?" asked Mr Yamamoto.

"No" replied Liu Chung. "Time is something that man has invented. Time for dragons does not exist. For them there is only 'Now' 'The Present'. The egg will remain dormant until a parent awakens it by breathing its fiery breath upon it. Then it should be kept warm by the parent by putting it in a special place under its throat."

Jamie looked again at the egg then said "But it's not in its parents place now. Wouldn't it die?"

Liu Chung smiled. " No, my young friend, it would take a lot of snow and ice to put out the fire of a dragon, but just to be sure, when I get back home I shall place the egg in the hottest furnace, of the hottest steel making plant, until it's time to hatch."

The rest of the journey home was uneventful. Grandad and Jamie were dropped off in the same place they were picked up. Jamie was bursting to tell his parents about his great adventure and when he burst through the front door he jabbered on and on about everything he had seen and done. Jamie's Mother looked at Jamie and said, "That's enough of that now young man. You can tell us all about your trip to the zoo with Grandad tomorrow. It's now your bedtime, so off you go." Jamie looked at her with incredulity. "Zoo?" ...Mom you haven't listened to a word I've been saying" said Jamie.

"And I said 'Bed Time," replied Jamie's Mom.

Jamie looked at Grandad. "Tell them Grandad," said Jamie.

Grandad just smiled back at Jamie. Gave a slow wink and then said. "Goodnight Son. See you in the morning."

Jamie just looked back at Grandad for a few seconds and then understood that it was pointless arguing. Jamie suddenly felt very weary. He then wished everyone goodnight Turned and trooped off up the stairs, undressed, showered and slumped in bed. The bed was soft and warm with the fresh smell of clean bedding. He closed his eyes and went instantly to sleep.

A short while later Jaime's Mom came up the stairs to check on him. She opened the door and peeped in. She noticed that Jamie had dumped his clothes on the bedroom door and crept in to pick them up. As she picked up his jeans, something fell out of his pocket and rolled across the floor, out of the door and out on to the landing. She then gathered the rest of Jamie's clothes and followed the coin out of the room. She then bent over and picked up the coin which had come to rest near the wall. It was a big gold coin, very heavy and looked very old. She stood and looked at it for a minute and had a quizzical look on her face. She thought about what Jamie had said and began to wonder. She then noticed Jamie's clothes had a damp feel to them as well as a funny 'musty' smell. Could it be that Jamie just might be telling the truth? ...She then banished the thought from her mind. She turned and went back into Jamie's room looked at him sleeping peacefully in his bed before placing the coin on the small bedside table, turned, and left the room closing the bedroom door very slowly and very quietly behind her.

THE END

52764434R00071

Made in the USA
Charleston, SC
28 February 2016